The Psychian Chronicles

The Psychian Chronicles

Book One:
The Kimoshiran Form

Timothy Bryant

Order this book online at www.trafford.com
or email orders@trafford.com

Most Trafford titles are also available at major online book retailers.

Printed in the United States of America.

ISBN: 978-1-4269-6788-7 (sc)
ISBN: 978-1-4269-6787-0 (e)

Trafford rev. 05/12/2011

www.trafford.com

North America & International
toll-free: 1 888 232 4444 (USA & Canada)
phone: 250 383 6864 ♦ fax: 812 355 4082

Chapter 1

My Oldest Friend Ruji

The sun is shining on a Friday morning, it's not a good day to wear black. My name is Shinruga Deshreneto and I have just completed the first part of my Psychian training. Psychian's an evolved race of the humans. Three races of Psychian's exists the Shogun, Kimoshiran, and the Psychian Warrior. A Psychian Warrior possesses more strength than the other two kinds of Physician's. A dark purple energy is what will tell us apart from the other two. That's what I was born and have mastered this form.

We Psychian's were born after the humans were nearly wiped from existence. Our ancestors are not sure what happened to the humans but know greed and power had something to do with the cause. They fear us because we are seventy percent the population. A great war has struck out once between the two kinds but that was almost one hundred and fifty years ago. The Triple Psychian's who's power compared to none, destroyed the humans who by name is the Apocalypse Unit. It came at a price though in the end he sacrificed himself to save his people.

I was walking to my house in the city of Recnamorcen, which if you look at backwards it spells out necromancer. Kind of odd but no one really pays attention to it. That's when I heard it my name being called from behind me.

"Hey, Shinruga"! Someone yells.

Ruji Thean, my best friend who was my training partner even though he was weaker than me.

"How was your training"? I asked.

"Okay". Ruji says.

Psychians train so that we can defeat humans who try to kill us. Most of them hate us, there is talk about them getting together and starting a war again. We also love a good fight; it's like a drug to us.

Most fights are more of sparring than a fight to the death.

"You seem different".Ruji says in a worried voice.

I remember back to the first time I met Ruji, I said the same about him it was a warm sunny day and are fathers had just got back from a mission. Before that I had not really known him but I remembered how he was before that day. The day he found out his father had died in battle. Soon after I talked to him for the first time and he seemed lost and dead. But after several weeks of us talking and becoming friends his eyes and mood went back to old. Now I see him high on his new found power. He's ready to defend himself with his cool manner. "I'm fine". I reply. I have changed though. Become more serious, not just some kid who doesn't have a care in the world.

When your parents think you're ready you're sent to a school of your Psychian kind and trained in the ways of their fighting. Fortunately for me my school was right in my home town. Ruji's school was in a town called Agno which trained Shogun's, there energy is the color red.

The point of these schools is to train us in case the humans attack again. Lately there have been more and more attacks on our people. Seven years ago my hometown of Shiran was attacked and nearly destroyed. We scared our enemies off and rejoiced in an era of peace. The threat of another looming war, only fuels our fire to train harder. While we wait for a new Triple Psychian to arise we fight our enemies off the best we can.

"You wanna spar"? Ruji asks.

"Why not"? I say. I was hoping he would ask it's been a couple of days since I have so I've been itching for some fighting.

"Let's do this". Ruji says.

Ruji charges but I anticipate the attack tripping him. I jump at him to put my foot into his stomach but he sees this coming as will. He charges up a blast of energy and hits me square in the chest.

"Ah". I cry out in pain as the energy hits me like a brick.

"Come on". Ruji yells.

I charge with energy powered hands and swing violently and the second punch hits Ruji, right in the gut. He staggers and I prepare my next assault of punches, but as I do Ruji uses one of his special attacks.

"Try this".

The next thing I see is what looks like a Phercon beast coming at me; it strikes me hard knocking me about twenty feet back.

Ruji's blade is the Phercon blade. It's a two handed sword orange and marked with Ruji's initials, the end of the blade is wavy and has a gut hook a quarter the way down on the back. To which is named after a beast in our time the Phercon. They are beast that lives in the wild untamed and unable to tame. They all look different from one another but are strong creatures, so naturally most of Ruji's attacks are going to center around a Phercon.

I stagger to get to my feet, feeling the full force of the tackle I just experienced.

"You think you can win with that Brigidane blade"?

My Brigidane blade given to me by my father it once held the Elemenka's orbs that would possess people and make them do unspeakable things this is my mission to find them and put them back in the blade.

"I'll try".

I charge up a fistful of energy and shoot it right at Ruji. He dodges sending the same special attack at me for the second time. Instead of being hit, this time I pour energy into my fist and spread it making a shield the beast slams into it disappearing.

"What else you got"? I ask.

But just as were about to charge and attack again were stopped by Priests Frederick.

Priests Frederick in his mid forties, he is my dad's best friend. He wears a turban and large robes. A thick beard covered his face an Ankh around his neck which I guess means life. Never cared for trinkets like that myself. He's not a Psychian but he has a lot of authority here at home.

"Well, look at you two all grown up". Frederick says. "I have a mission for each of you Shinruga your mission is to go and find the men who beat your father".

Frederick must see the anger and worry in my eye because he's quick to assure me that my father is all right.

"What direction"? I ask.

"That one if you use the element of surprise you should be able to beat them they did the same to your father, they were looking for your sword, here's a brief description of what they look like". Frederick says. "Ruji, I want you to go to Silver Lake City and watch the Roko gang but do not engage them in battle. This is simply surveillance".

"Yes sir". Ruji yells.

The Roko gang, gang of Psychians who think they can do whatever they want. Some think that the humans who might be forming together to start a war again, are working with the Roko gang. My father and his friend helped defeat the Roko gang a long time ago but I guess they're back and stronger than ever.

"Looks like we'll have to postpone our little match".

"Guess so". I reply back. As we're leaving we exchange a gesture with our hands. Looking into Ruji's eyes I remember seeing his expression calm and sure of himself and that we will see each other again.

Being a Psychian there's some advantages one of them is placing your blade on the ground and it will hover. After that you can ride on it like a vehicle.

It's nearing night time now and I see the faint flicker of a flame coming from the woods. I get in as close as possible without them noticing me, there are five of them. They match the descriptions.

"I need to think strategically". I whisper to myself. It takes me a few minutes but I finally come up with an idea. I place five balls of energy around them in a circle but not using too much energy so that I don't threaten my enemy. When they're in place I clench my open hand into a fist, the energy explodes the five immediately stand up poised for battle. I swoop down knocking out two of them the other three faces me two of them slash at me with their swords. I block one with energy in my one hand and the other with my sword.

"Who are you"? Ask their leader with rage.

"Shinruga Deshreneto". I reply. I can see their leader enraged by my sneak attack; it was quite clever but no time to soak in the glory.

"Oh good now I don't have to track you down, names Ebon and I want that blade". He says.

"What for"? I ask. There's nothing really special to it just a mission that'll waste your time. That I never wanted in the first place.

Ebon has seen many battles so far, that's for sure. He's huge probably six-five, he has big scars on his stomach, very muscular but he doesn't frighten me.

"Fool, just by absorbing the gems into the sword it will increase your power. Has your father told you nothing about this sword"? Ebon barks.

That's me, don't listen to anyone he probably told me but I didn't listen as usual. I just saw the sword as another chore, to capture the gems.

"Attack"! Ebon yells as the two come at me again.

I flip backwards at the same time shooting two blasts at the enemies. Not hitting them though instead I hit the fire it explodes, blinding all three and burning the two henchmen's backs. They cry out in pain, but Ebon is not impressed.

"Pretty clever"! Ebon shouts. He unsheathes his sword. "Prepare to face doom".

"You can try". I told him.

We charge at each other and lock swords but he's so strong he's forcing me to the ground where he will surely finish me. Drive the cold of his steel into my chest.

As I'm sure of my imminent doom is about to happen a blast hits Ebon in the back. Ebon falls to my right when I look up I'm greeted by the sight of Septh.

Septh one of the strongest Psychian, his normal size and his rigid eyes but power beyond belief. He won every tournament he's ever been in never been beaten. He's known as the gifted child. He's not a child anymore late twenties.

"Shinruga, your friend Ruji needs your help". Septh says calmly.

"Thanks for the help but I could of handled them...How do you know he needs my help"? I ask.

"I'm sure you could of...Go Ruji is in danger". Septh instructs.

I was hoping that he was wrong but I'm getting a bad feeling in my stomach. Like I'm about to throw up, is he hurt or worse. No I couldn't imagine my best friend being dead.

I arrive in Silver Lake City the next morning exhausted. Apparently there's a tournament going on today, this was where Ruji was supposed to spy on the Roko gang. It's a scene of pandemonium hundreds of Psychians and people, come to watch the event of course. I've never been to one of these before my father feared I would be a target for his enemies and that I could be hurt or killed. I scour the place looking for Ruji; I look for about an hour or two…Nothing.

With my spare time I sign up for the tournament. There's three levels of the tournament a beginners level a intermediate and an expert level. So the tournament officials can tell which level to put you in they have a machine. You put your hand in and put out as much energy as possible; it registers how much and puts you in the coordinated level.

We have these tournaments to find out who's the most powerful. They were formed a long time ago sometime after the Triple Psychian was killed. I think that there's some kind of hidden agenda behind them, as if someone's watching the tournaments sizing us up.

As I look and look for Ruji I come to a shady group of people. Who has the mark of the Roko gang stamped on the back of their shirts? A round dark circle with the figure of a man black with red eyes is their mark, the mark of pure evil. They are ruthless and evil they don't care about life just as long as they get what they want. They've attacked my hometown a couple of times my dad of course took care of them quickly.

Something catches my eye though; when I look back I notice it. It's Ruji's sword. I'm filled with rage and power, I feel like walking up and stabbing him in the back. I realize that I would be just as bad as they would be.

"Roca, behind you"! I hear one of the gang members say.

Roca is tall brown hair and his face has a scar going from the side of the neck to them middle of the cheek. It's his eyes that confuse me they're not completely dark or evil like the rest of the members in the group. Roca is the only one not wearing the patch or a jacket with symbol of the Roko gang on him. I find that kind of odd because he's the leader of the group.

He turns to face me and that's when I notice a little hint of fear in his eyes and a kind of excitement.

"Shinruga, been a while". Roca says.

"Do I know you"? I ask.

"Roca…Sounni's friend"? He exclaims. "You came to her house a couple of times when I was there, about ten years ago".

"I remember now". I say. When my dad would go see his friend, his daughter would be there too. We would play and every once in a while her friend Roca would come over. We would all play and be happy, good old times I say.

"Where's my friend Ruji"? I demand.

"Wouldn't you like to know"? Says one of the members. "Go check the woods and you would know. Not sure you want to see though".

I hope for the best but it's not likely that he will be ok. As I'm leaving I catch Roca's eyes they show fear. The worst thing I could hope to see.

As I get to the woods I search and search when I see it the outline of a body. Is it please no, no I can feel my body getting weak, my legs feel as if they have a thousand pounds on them. I inch closer and closer to the body, fearing that it is him I stop for a second. I stop to catch my breath and try to ready myself in case it is him.

I get to the body finally and then I see him it is Ruji, his frail limp body lying there cold. Alone and waiting for life to be brought back to it. I look at the body closely and notice a wound; I have a flashback of the group of Roko gang members. I remember one of them having a blade of the same style as the wound. I get up and start running back to the tournament and ready myself to go back to the tournament grounds to prepare for my vengeance.

My worst fear it's realized my best friend is dead Ruji is dead. RUJI IS DEAD!And now I have to avenge his death.

"I will avenge you and I will come back for your body".

CHAPTER TWO

THE TOURNAMENT

I arrive back at the tournament grounds and find Roca and his group of men.

"Which one of you killed him"? I shout in anger.

"Who do you think"? says the one who gave me the hint to check the woods.

I'm about ready to attack him when a tournament official comes behind us. He tells us all that there is no fighting except for is assigned fights by the tournament.

"I'll see you after the tournament". I say to him.

We all get back to spot where the other fighters have joined up. Some of them are muscular and others skinnier like me. When it comes to Psychian's though it's not about size it's about how skilled a fighter you are.

While standing there waiting for the results, trying to figure out who I have to fight a man comes up to me. He's about six feet tall and has long black hair, wearing some type of formal suit from earths past. He has a scar on his right cheek; I'm surprised that he's here because you can definitely that he's human.

"Shinruga". He asks.

I'm not surprised that he knows my name, most people know my name. My father is one the most famous Psychian's in history he designed the blade that I'm holding. The one that captured the Elemenka gems. The Elemenka gems are put into a blade and the Psychian is turned into pure evil, the Brigidane blade turns the evil into power for the user. My father killed each of the fighters and captured the gems but about six months ago someone broke into our house and stole them. The Elemenka's caused chaos for years; even though it wasn't their fault people still were mad at them. They were unstoppable killing humans and Psychians alike my father and his friend Furrock killed them.

"Yes, who are you"? I reply. Trying to dissect what possible thing reason he has for wanting to come to me.

"Kita, I was wondering if I could have a few minutes with you please". Says Kita.

"I guess". I say.

"I just wanted to say good luck on your matches and ask if you've found any of the Elemenka gems yet". He asks.

"No". I say. It wouldn't be that weird for a human to ask this question just as well as a Psychian because of the devastation they caused everyone."They could be anywhere, it could take a while. I'm here on business".

"I see. Keep up the good work. Don't die either, the humans and Psychian's are counting on you". Kita says.

I give him a weird kind of look and I think he sees it. It's because of the way he said don't die, it sounds almost sarcastic and evil at the same time. He waves his hand as he's walking with his back to me.

That's when I hear it my name being called again by one of the tournament officials. When I get there, I see the machine that registers energy it's clear and conforms to your hand when you put it in it. It has a type of machine on the top I suppose it tells the tournament officials what your energy level is. I'm right and when it shows my level it's just a little over four hundred. I look over and notice that Roca's on the machine across from me and his level is around four hundred and ninety. He looks at me still with those eyes of innocence and regret, but he's still part of the Roko gang that makes him evil. We wait for the results to come in for who we verse in our matches. You have three matches in the tournament.

The results come in; my first match is with someone named Slay. The one who laughed about Ruji, his killer. I can picture him laughing as he stabs Ruji in his heart.

I'm standing there mulling over what I will do to him when Roca's first opponent Shokon comes up to me, by looking at his clothes I suppose he's probably a shogun.

"Looks like Roca's my first opponent". Says Shokon.

"Looks like it". I say. Shokon has long hair down to his neck; he has the shogun patch on his right arm and dressed in traditional Japanese armor with one shoulder pad on his left shoulder. He also has a couple of knives in little sheaths on his chest. I notice something in his hand; it's the Roko gang insignia.

"After I saw them kill your friend for that blade I told them I quit". He says.

He must have seen my eyes looking at it.

"They would've killed me as well if you want revenge Slay will be your opponent he has a horse sword, a lot of charging attacks."

I can't exactly figure out why he helped but I'm grateful.

Shokon

My name is Shokon; I come from a town called Porter. It was nearly wiped out by the Roko gang and since then I have had no choice but to join them. It has taken me twelve long years but today the day of the tournament, where I saw them kill Shinruga's friend is the day I quit. So I walk up the stairs to the place where I know Kita will be. It's a dark room at the top of the stairs overlooking the ring for the tournament. As I get up to the door the two guards who block it get in the way.

"Let me in now". I announce. They do and when I open the door I can see Kita sitting in front of a window, which can see the ring.

"What can I do for you Shokon"? Kita asks.

"I quit, I'm out". I say. He doesn't look mad or even a little upset even. Strangely the woman behind him, with the scar on her right eye is more upset, but he waves for her to calm down.

"Interesting you come in here saying you quit by yourself, what's to say I won't kill you right here and now"? He asks.

I take my hand out of my pocket and hold them out a handful of small grenades. He still doesn't seem too worried.

"That might do it". He says. "You can leave if you want but know this you will be hunted till the day you die. Every single Roko gang member will want your head".

"They can try". I snap back.

"Guards escort him out". He bellows.

As I'm walking down the stairs I feel a rush of freedom and drop the insignia to the ground.

"That's for you little brother". I whisper.

Back to Shinruga

I wait for my match, my anticipation grows but it will have to wait a few more minutes. I have to wait for the tournament announcer to get through his speech. He's obviously not a fighter or even a Psychian; he looks to be about mid forties, blond hair and tall. He's rambling on about what tournament number this is and how he's congratulating all the fighters for coming out. He's annoying to me because I'm just waiting for my match with Slay.

"It won't bring him back you know". Says Shokon who has somehow snuck behind me.

"I know". I say. "But he was my best friend and to be killed for something so feeble and small, deserves vengeance".

"I never actually killed anyone unless I had to". He says. "But the people I did I can still see their faces".

"So what are you asking me…Not to kill him"? I ask.

"Just wondering could you live with yourself, and know that you're still a good person"? He questions. "I thought I could and it's hard to get through some days".

"Thanks for the advice but I'll be okay". I say.

That's when I hear the tournament announcer call mine and Slay's name. As were walking up to the ring I can see that smile of Slay's creep along his mouth. He's ugly big brown eyes they're uneven, by the look of his hair he hasn't washed in a while, eyes dark and evil.

"Hopefully you're stronger than he is". He says.

I'm enraged and now I know that I'm ready for this match. As we walk into the middle of the ring the announcer asked for a word from the both of us.

"So Shinruga this is your first tournament, you're finally stepping out of your father's shadow. How does it feel"? He asks. "And what do you think of your opponent"?

"My father was great but I will be greater and as far as my opponent goes he's dirt". I shout with a sinful tone.

"And you Slay"? Ask the announcer.

"He's a hack".

I think to myself if I'm a hack what is he, DIRT. That's the word that comes to mind. We take are fighting poses as the announcer readies us for battle.

"Fight". The announcer shouts.

He charges fast, incredibly fast like a horse. He puts both fist out and I block them by grabbing both fist. I throw him across the ring. He flips backwards and shoots an energy blast. I pull out my sword and cut it in half. I put my sword away and charge and up a huge energy blast and shoot. He uses his energy and puts a chunk of earth in front of himself. Psychians can manipulate any element and about anything with their energy. I shoot a couple of energy blast, none of them hit. I'm about to charge another energy attack, when stuff around Slay comes out around the ground. They're in the shapes of horses made of earth.

"What the"? I'm stunned at what he's created.

I shoot an energy blast at one it does nothing. So instead I pull out my sword and as they charge I slash them in half. One gets too close and knocks me to the ground. The next thing I see is a giant earth hoof coming straight at my face, thinking as fast as I can I slap my hand to the ground. Sending an earth spike through the horse's stomach, it turns to rubble.

"I didn't think you were going to survive that". He says. As the grin creeps across his face again and I realize I hate him even more.

"I won't lose that easily".

I won't lose I can't lose not for Ruji's memory. This is it my turn to strike to show what I got. I power up some energy and use an attack that makes a box of energy around him. With bars like a prison and white and multicolored balls of life energy at each corner.

Life energy is our reserves twice as strong as our regular energy but drains much faster. The humans say it's your soul, Psychians don't believe in the afterlife. If your life energy runs out, you're dead.

"Touch it you're dead". I explain. "Touch it and the whole thing blows". I'm about to explain it to him when he tries to escape so I close my fist and blow the box of energy up. I look for any signs of him but there is too much dust in the way. When the dust clears to my surprise he's still there. I get ready to fight again, but I notice that Slay is dazed by the explosion. Now is the best time to attack. I charge ready to engage in battle when I stop. He's starting to grow horse legs and before I can do anything he's half horse.

"Now let's see what you can do"? He says. He charges and he's so fast that I just barely miss getting hit by the hoofed creature.

I shoot energy at him but all he does is bat it away. I dodge him and he jumps in front of me and kicks his right leg, hitting me in the gut. Luckily I put energy over the spot as not to damage anything internally. The hit makes me bounce and fly into the air; I pull out my sword and stab it into the ground. It stops me just before I go out of the ring; I sit there panting from the hit waiting for him to charge again. I charge up an enormous energy attack, it hits him dead on. The smoke clears and he seems fine, not even scathed. I'm seeking a way to beat my opponent when he rushes. I instinctively throw up my sword and he puts his hoofs down on my sword. He's trying to crush me; he's almost there when I move my right foot tripping his back feet. As he's falling over I roll out of the way. I don't wait even a second to strike I jump up slashing at him with my sword, but he unsheathes his blade striking me down. Cutting my arm, I fall to the ground. I look at the gaping wound on my arm, the searing pain hits me.

"You thought you had me". He says. "Does it hurt"?

I snipe back claiming it doesn't but it does I can feel it burning, and bleeding. I place my hand with some energy to the wound. It's going to take a while to heal, but I got to take care of him first anyways. What can I do I ask myself? He charges again I'm not exactly ready for him but I manage, I use earth to grab his front two feet and he flips over me. I cut his back right leg. He cries out in pain but is on his feet quickly and still manages to come at me almost just as fast. I shoot energy up into the sky and when he's close enough I bring my arm down sending a bolt of lightning to the ground. It hits just in front of us, it knocks us both back.

"Did it work"? I wonder, but as the smoke clears I see he's not dead. He's out of his centaur form; I can see the sparks coming around his body. I don't seem to hurt by the lightning but my wound on my arm is only getting worse. He's getting up slowly, it will only be a little bit more time till his body will recover from the lightning.

"That kind of stung a little bit". Slay says with a groan.

"Keep fighting and the pain will keep coming". I say with arrogance.

He looks fine now and I can feel his power rising and he fires a huge blast of energy. I easily dodge it; I think it was his plan the whole time. Two more horses of earth of come to my right and left, I move forward. I'm about three steps ahead when the two horses collide and become one and charge, I flip backwards with my sword and slash it in half.

"You think you can keep it up forever"? I ask. I don't think he can he's already looking fatigued but I'm not doing so great myself.

"Ahhh"! Slay's coming quick he's mad like a bull.

I wait and when he comes in close enough trip him up. He rapidly turns and swings with his right arm I kick with my right leg in his head, knocking his right arm down. I keep swinging landing blow after blow, I put both my hands together charging energy, hitting him in the jaw. He cries out in pain and flies across the ring he uses his energy to manipulate the air and float down.

I need to hurry because my energy is low and only getting lower. Now's my time to end this, I run as fast as possible toward my enemy. I stop right before I get to him he's about to attack when I use the earth to make a wall behind him. When he looks back I unleash a huge energy blast, hitting him directly I keep going pouring out everything I have. He's yelling and when I stop he collapses to the ground.

"No there's no way you won". He Slay says. "It's not possible I can't let you win, you're a weakling compared to me".

"Really". I say. I pull up my blade to strike him I can see the look in his face the fear in his eyes I strike but I don't stab him.

"Fool, weakling you're pathetic". He says.

"I'm not you…A killer". I explain.I'm walking away from him I have my back to him and that's when I sense him, he's inches from me when I pull up my sword and stab him in his neck. His face, his eyes wide and dead. I pull out my blade and use a rag to clean it off.

I'm walking out of the ring and into the lobby where all the other fighters are. That's when I see him Shokon he's staring at me.

"Sorry, I didn't want to kill him". I say with displease. "He came at me I had no choice".

"I know he's avenged now you can let it go".

"I will thank you Shokon". I'm grateful for what he told me but I have my vengeance now, there only one more thing to do. Get Ruji's blade back and get his body back home. I lay on one of the beds in the lounge, listening to the tournament announcer chanting for the next two fighters to come to ring. The chanting of the people waiting for their entertainment to start.

I awake from my sleep just in time to see that Shokon's match is just about to start. I'm still a little fatigued from my match but I'll manage.

The tournament announcer asks them a question before their match starts.

"Shokon, is it true that you have quit the Roko gang"? The announcer asks.

"Yes". He replies.

"Roca what do you have to say to this"? He asks.

"Shokon knows what I have to do". Roca says with regret.

The announcer tells them both to get ready to fight. When they take their fighting poses the announcer calls for them both to fight. Instantly they both charge at each other and start exchanging blows. Shokon uses his energy to suck water from every available source he can, and turns the water into spikes of ice. He shoots them at Roca who dodges a few of them and slices the rest onto the ring. I'm surprised at how fast Roca is for his size. He charges up an attack and uses to fire to make snakes and sends them Shokon's way. Shokon jumps up into the air, avoiding the attack and powering up a huge blast. He shoots it hitting Roca right in the face, it seems like it hardly fazes Roca. Whose head just bends backwards a little bit? Roca then sends the fiery snakes back at Shokon. They hit him and Shokon disappears into a burst of flames.

"Shokon". I yell out. I'm worried, because I don't see any sign of life. Just as the announcer is about to call Roca the winner, the flames blow away. Shokon is there with an energy shield around him close to his body the closest I've ever seen a Psychian make.

"Thought you were a goner for a second". Says Roca. He's ready poised for battle.

"Not a chance".

They go back at it again energy flying in all directions, and taking blow after blow from one another. Shokon jumps back and charges up energy in his hand and shoots them they miss Roca completely.

"What was that"? Roca asks. Shokon attacks with speed and fury, I can tell that Roca wasn't ready for it as he's knocked back by the first hit. Then Shokon backs off the two blasts he fired earlier hits Roca, one at his leg the other at his head. It sends him in a spin in midair. He stops spinning and hits the ground with a big thud.

"Give up Roca". Shouts Shokon. Shokon's ready for another attack and waits patiently for Roca to get up. When he does he doesn't look to hurt but furious his expression has changed from and arrogant and happy looking to mad, psychotic almost. He's charging now and zigzagging Shokon's energy, Shokon fires in the middle Roca jumps. When he comes down he hits Shokon right in the head, then a swing with his left. Hitting Shokon across the cheek charging up energy in his knee he nails Shokon right in the gut, I could hear him groan and the breaking of a bone.

Shokon falls to his knees but instead of Roca slicing his head off or stabbing him, he just walks away. The announcer yells that the match is over and Shokon starts walking toward me. I help him walk all the way to the bench.

"I couldn't beat him". He says.

"Don't worry about it man". I say. "I'll get him I have to, to get Ruji's sword back".

"You better". "He can't be turned to their side; if he sees what they do he'll want out. Them killing your friend shocked him he's not evil like they are".

Shokon drifts off not even being able to finish his last sentence. I prepare myself for the next match and as I'm standing there one of the holes on the bottom of my sword starts lighting up. I remember what my father says this means it means one of the Elemenka gems is nearby. It's glowing more and more as I walk in a certain direction and just when I think I'm close it's gone. I turn the corner to see if there is anyone there, nothing and the glowing has stopped. I was so close to it, my first Elemenka gem. I can hear him now the announcer calling my name for my second match. I walk toward the direction of the ring ready to fight.

Chapter 3

Shinruga vs. Roca

Nosabe is suppressing his power I can feel almost no energy coming from him. His demeanor is calm and cool headed. The announcer once again ask us for a statement. I say only one thing to my opponent! "I hope he's ready for the fight of his life".

"And what do you have to say to that Nosabe"? Asks the annonuncer.

"I sure hope so".

"Well then let the match begin". Yells the announcer at the top of his lungs.

We both get into fighting position and wait for the announcer to begin the match.

"Fight"! He yells.

I charge as fast as I can and throw up my right fist, Nosabe dodges it. He kicks with his right leg I flip backwards with one hand and shooting a blast of energy with my other. It hits Nosabe in his chest but it hardly fazes him, he uses his hand and arm to send a wave of earth at me. I jump to my left and avoid the earth wave shooting two more energy blast at him, when I touch ground I charge up one big blast of energy. Instead of dodging the two blasts or getting hit by them like I predicted would happen, he rips off his turban and cuts it in half. The Turban pieces each grab one blast and throws it at the big blast.

"Surprised"? He asks. As he's wrapping each one of the pieces of turban around his wrist. "This turban is infused with pure energy".

"I figured so". I say. I wait till he's done wrapping the pieces of turban around his wrist anticipating every move he could possibly make.

It takes a minute for Nosabe but he dashes at me with lightning speed. I do my best to avoid his new weapons but he catches the side of my face with his second attempt, knocking me into the air. The pain is excruciating but I'm glad it's not a sword. Nosabe goes to my side slashing downwards I spin releasing energy bouncing him back. I pull out my sword and slash but he grabs it with the turban pieces. We struggle to get my sword, Nosabe lets go with his right weapon and pulls as hard as he can with his left.

He punches with his right fist and the turban piece afterwards. I fall to the ground clenching my left cheek. My blade spins in the air and goes outside the ring and sticks in the wall.

"I thought you were stronger than this"? He says. "A few hits and you fall and whimper like a little girl".

"I'm not done trust me on that". I yell.

I bang my hands onto the ground and cover it in earth. Then I send some to my face and some parts of my body. I dash as quickly as I can, even though the earth around me is dramatically slowing me down. I try to land a series of blows but he's too quick. He slashes with his turbans but the earth is doing a pretty good job of fending off the strikes. He grabs both my arms, I don't let him hit me though I jump up and kick him in the face. It knocks him about five feet back I don't falter I charge again punching downward. I miss him hitting the ground, he slashes at my head. I throw up my hands to block his attack; he kicks out my left leg knocking me to my knees. The turbans wrap around my arm and Nosabe tries to pull and throw me but I use my energy to plant myself to the ground. The turbans start wrapping around me more. When I can't move anymore Nosabe starts punching my face. After a few hits I'm about to pass out, I can't lose though. I pour out as much energy as possible to break the hold of the turbans, it works I put all my strength into my fist and hit Nosabe right in the gut. I can hear his rib break as he goes flying across the ring. I'm on one knee trying to regain composure but Nosabe is already at my face with his turban. I roll to my right jump backwards shooting energy blast after energy blast. It does no good, he jumps up with me wraps the turbans around my legs and grabs my arms and knees me in the stomach three times. I fall to the ground hardly able to breathe.

"Come on Shinruga I thought you were at least going to be a challenge"? He ask. "So far all you've done is disappointed me".

Once again he comes at me but before he gets to me I use the earth to make a statue of me. Nosabe cuts it in half with his turbans. Before he can even think to make a move I strike with my right fist as hard as I can to the left side of his face. He does a complete three-sixty and tries to decapitate me at the same time, he misses. I blast him with some energy knocking him onto the ground. I go to attack but the turbans start spinning cutting the ground as Nosabe is walking. There's only one thing that could expect to block it my sword, still stuck in the wall. Nosabe can sense what I want his attention immediately goes to my sword as well. I start booking it towards my sword but Nosabe is right next to me. Trying to hit me with his weapon, I can't expect to get it if he's right there. Using energy I bring up earth everywhere around him and enclose him in it. I run out of the ring and grab the sword but it just won't come out.

"Come on". I yell. It won't come out and I expect Nosabe will be out of that earthly coffin in no time. Next there is an explosion and Nosabe is standing there with a furious look on his face.

"That's it I'm finishing this right now". He yells. He barrels at me with god like speed. I yank on the sword but it won't budge.

"Just come out". I yell out in aggravation. The sword finally comes out of the wall, with Nosabe still charging I point the end of my sword at him. It hits the spinning turban pieces and Nosabe wraps them around my sword and throws me back into the ring. He barrels at me again with his weapons straight like blades. He strikes at me with a series of blows, he's about to hit me but I pull my swords sheathe off of its string and block the attack. It's not long before I notice that my sheathe has deep cuts in it, it won't be long till Nosabe cuts through it. I could make a sword or shield out of energy but it would be no use I would have to keep adding to it. I throw up my sword to block with my sword but the sheathe gets cut clean through, he barely misses me. While his weapon is down I swing my left arm and hit Nosabe in the face with my elbow.

"Augh". He cries out.

I don't stop, flipping my sword around and stab his left shirt sleeve into the ground. Using my left hand to hold his other hand, I start punching him in the face. Nosabe's about to pass out, when he starts pouring energy out of him. I try to punch him again but the energy field around him is to strong.

"There's no way I'm going to let some little punk kid like you beat me". He barrels at me with an exploding force.

"Bring it". I reply. Charging up energy I pound my fist on the ground and send a wave of earth towards him. He jumps over it, I send a piece of earth flying and Nosabe doesn't see it in time. It sends him flying backwards he hits the ground with an immense force. My body is killing me and I can barely hold my arms up and my legs feel giggly. The anticipation is getting to me; Nosabe is taking a long time to get up. I fall to one knee that's when Nosabe starts to get up. He's staggering though almost like he's about to die.

"These turbans may be as strong as or stronger than any sword but it takes a lot of energy out of you". Nosabe clarifies. "Not so much energy but life energy".

"That's dangerous". I warn him but he doesn't seem to listen he just rolls his eyes. I get back into fighting pose ready for him to run at me with a new attack. Nosabe starts to charge but I stop him dead in his tracks, with one of my best moves the Implosion Box. The box of energy has eight corners of life energy, and bars of energy to enclose Nosabe in.

"Interesting attack". He says.

"Touch one of the bars or the corners and it will explode and don't even think about going underground because it's under there to". I explain. "As you can see it's getting smaller and smaller but I can squeeze my hand into a fist and it will also make it explode".

"Interesting if I still had my turbans it would've been easy to get out of this". He claims with arrogance. "Yet I still can even without them".

It takes me a second to realize that he's telling the truth. Before I can take in the thought Nosabe raises a slab of earth behind him and uses his feet to springboard off of it and through the boxes bars. I squeeze my fingers into a fist; the explosion barely catches him and hurts his back. Nosabe falls on his knees and yells out in pain. I'm about to charge at Nosabe again but before I can he gives up.

"I give up my body can't take no more". He says.

The tournament announcer rushes into the ring. Puts the microphone up to Nosabe's mouth and insist that Nosabe yells his forfeit to the crowd.

"Do you really give up Nosabe"? He asks in his usual persistent manner.

"Yes, I can't continue no more. My body is far too exhausted, Shinruga is the winner". Nosabe answers.

"Well what a fight". The announcer grabs my arm throws it up and announces my win. The crowd goes wild Psychians and humans alike.

I walk off the ring, exhausted and about to pass out. My eagerness takes over, it's Roca's turn to fight and I want to see his fight. We pass each other in the hall, the tension is overbearing.

"You're going to need better moves than that to beat me". He says. "The Roko gang wants me to kill you".

"Well do you want to"? I ask.

"No, given are past I don't like you but not enough to want to kill you". He says. "I never wanted to kill anyone".

"What do you think the Roko gang do"? I say with aggravation. I'm annoyed at how stupid he sounds; everyone knows what the Roko gang does.

"There's only one way out Shinruga and you know that…By death". He explains.

The announcer calls Roca's name to the ring. I can't help feeling that he doesn't really want to fight, given the expression he gives me when he hears his name called. He walks to the ring with a smile and his usual look of confidence on his face. Luckily this is my last fight for the day. The final match takes place the next day so that the fighters are fully healed. So that the crowd gets a good show. I want to find the nearest bench and just fall asleep but my curiosity gets to me. I lean against the doorway watching Roca. The announcer calls for the match to start and the second he does Roca is at his opponent. Landing fist after fist across his face, Roca's opponent pulls out his sword and so does Roca deflecting it. Roca charges up a handful of energy and blast his opponent. As I'm sitting there watching Roca, Shokon comes up to me.

"Are you ready to fight him, you're watching him right now. He's vicious with his attacks and still can keep his concentration". He says. "You're going to have to rely on luck more than anything".

"I'll be okay". I reply. I watch as Roca pummels his opponent, blow after blow. Roca grabs his opponents head and slams it into the ground. The announcer once again rushes into the ring and calls for the fight to be over. Roca steps off the ring and the crowd cheers. He walks past me a little bit and stops.

"You could barely beat Nosabe, how do you even expect to lay a finger on me"? He asks. "Remember there's only one way to get me out I have to die or you do. For some reason the Roko Gang has their eye on you. Especially that blade of yours they think it has a lot of possibilities, I'm supposed to kill you and take it".

"Interesting, absorbing the Elemenka gems into the blade would increase mine and its power ten fol. We'll see who wins tomorrow; no one will ever get this sword". I say.

"Get some sleep now". He says.

I walk back to my room on the other side of the tournament. The audience members shuffle out of the stadium, and into their tents. Tournament members get their own rooms; sometime after I'm all situated Shokon comes into my room.

"Roca's left leg was hurt in a sparring accident a couple of years ago, too much pressure and it will give way". He tells me. "How is your father doing"?

I'm shocked when he asks me, not too many people should know it only happened yesterday.

"Thanks for the tip, but how'd you know about my father"? I ask.

"Your father was the Roko's gang first mark; they thought that he had the Brigidane blade. So they attacked him first when they realized he didn't have it, they were looking for you that's when they saw your friend. They knew they could get to you through him. I'm sorry about your friend I really am, for what it's worth he wouldn't tell them where you were".

"Thank you Shokon can you please go now"? I ask. My night is filled with nightmares and dreams of Ruji. My only true friend, I can see him fighting. Using every last bit of energy he has to stay alive but in the end he still falls. I can see him on the ground with his opponent's foot in his back. The Roko gang threatening to kill him, telling him if he doesn't tell them where I am they'll kill him. I am crying out now for Ruji, but I wake up and now I realize I am crying. I wipe my tears and realize it is daytime now. Ten o'clock in the morning, one hour till the fight. I notice some kid about fourteen years old walking around, scavenging more like. He's peering into bags and poking around into things. I walk up to him and get his attention.

"What are you doing"? I ask him.

"You're Shinruga, nothing just checking around for food". He says, even though I think he's lying.

"Here's some food".

I hand him some of my mom's homemade food and he runs off. Maybe he was after food but I wasn't going to chance him stealing and losing a hand or worse. It's about ten and I'm walking through the empty corridors when I see Kita and someone else but I can't quite make out who the other figure is. My ears can't tell what exactly they are saying, but I can pick up some of it.

"Is the Roko gang cooperating with you and your men"? Asks the hooded man in the corner.

"Yes, without question. They obey your every command and now mine". Kita replies with arrogance.

"Is operation Pokerian still going along as it should"?

"Yes, even better than we thought it would the Psychian's have gave up on resisting my forces? Word has not got out yet and Psychians still come in not...".

"Quiet someone's listening".

I duck behind the pillar beside me, and hear the hooded figure say that he is leaving. I peer back to the two of them and see the hooded man seem to disappear into the shadows. Kita starts walking back towards my way. I hide behind the pillar again hoping that Kita won't see me, he's just barely past me when he stops.

"Good luck on your match today Shinruga, hope you do okay". Kita says in a cold and sarcastic voice.

I don't know how but he seen me, and a cold chill goes down my back. I wait for Kita to go out of the doorway and into the arena and then I do as well. When I come out, people are starting to take their seats in the arena. Its ten thirty I go back to my room to get my stuff, with the basic weapons a Psychian will hold. A handful of kunai, couple of smoke bombs, and of course your sword. An extension of your arm, and a Psychian's best friend. I hurry and make a simple sheathe out of what's left of my old one.

I can hear the tournament announcer calling me and Roca to the ring. When I arrive Roca is already there with his arms folded and his usual smirk on his face. He nods his head into a direction and I look that way. I can't tell what he's nodding at though.

"What is it"? I ask.

"Sounni's here".

I look again and notice a woman a very beautiful woman, one like I've never seen before.

"She came to watch".

The announcer asks us both to come by him and ask us both to say a little word. I go first.

"My opponent better hope he's got some luck on his side". I say.

"Funny I was going to say the same about you". He says with a little chuckle. "Let's get this going before I die of old age".

The announcer calls for us both to get into fighting position and calls for the match to start.

The second the match starts Roca charges like a bull. He throws his right fist like a train that can't be stopped but I throw up my two fist block the punch. Roca throws his left fist and I jump up and block it with my right knee and swing my left foot across his face. Any normal opponent it would've sent flying but not Roca he takes it like it was almost nothing. It just knocks him a few feet back, and he comes at me once again. I can't fend off all his blows though, I block about three of his twenty hits. He knocks me up in the air with an uppercut to the jaw, I do a back flip and my feet grind against the ground. Roca's hot on my tail, I throw up my right foot and it hits Roca in the chin. I hit with both my fist as many times as possible. Roca grabs both my fist and extends his legs, both his feet connect with my face. I fall to my right knee clenching my face. Roca barely misses me as I jump back firing energy blasts to keep him back. When my vision returns blurry but still there, he throws out his right arm. I grab his arm with my hand and throw him over my shoulder. I put energy into my hand and punch at him on the ground. Roca rolls backwards kicks up his one foot and sends a pillar of earth into my fist. The explosion of energy and dirt goes into my face, I try to feel out Roca but I'm too distracted. A sword departs from a sheathe, my ears pick it up just in time and pull my blade out and block his strike.

"Give it up Shinruga". Roca says.

"Yeah, right".

His blade is coming closer to my face but I swing my foot and sweep his left leg. Roca kicks his left leg I block with my left arm. He charges up some energy in his left hand. I spring backwards as Roca fires his blast of energy. When I touch ground I extend my hand out and send a wave of earth at Roca, and in the other charge up energy. Roca jumps up and evades the earth wave and throwing multiple blast of energy at me. With the energy in hand I throw it up in front of his blast, the explosion puts me on my back and knocks the wind out of me. Before I have any time to rest Roca's already got some energy in his hands. He fires it at me I shoot some energy towards the sky. Before the blast can hit me I bring my arm down and lightning strikes it. I get up with energy charged in both hands.

"You've lasted a lot longer than I thought you would". Roca says. "You can take a hit, running low on energy yet"?

"Got plenty in me don't worry about that Roca".

"Ready to go again"? He asks.

I nod my head wondering how much longer I will last. He is right I am running low but I'll keep going till I fall over and can't get up. We run at each other hands charged and ready to kill. We both punch at each other, the energies collide and explode. I and Roca are sent backwards grinding against the ground. I make fire from the sparks and send it in Roca's direction. I wait till I think the fire get's in his line of sight to where he can't see me. Then I jump at Roca to punch him, his vision just catches me and he jumps up with energy in hand. I push off the ground with energy and tackle Roca before he can fire off his blast. I use energy to create a stand and fire off a blast. Roca summons a giant flaming snake, the blast goes through it and is heading in Roca's direction. He rolls backwards getting missed by just inches. I dash at him once again kicking at his head but he just crouches a little and my attack misses. Roca uppercuts my chin, which about knocks me out cold. When I land I see two blast of energy coming my way. I quickly grab the ground below me and toss two rocks, and destroy the blast.

"Implosion box". I yell out to stop Roca from firing his third blast.

Clenching my fist as fast as I can, ensuring that Roca can't find a way out. Before it collapses on him Roca summons two snakes to guard him from the explosion but he's not all the way shielded. When the smoke clears I can see him. On the ground and barely able to get up I poise ready for battle.

"Come on Roca". I holler at him. He can barely get up, and his energy level has definitely dropped.

"Come on now get up and fight". I yell at him again.

He gets himself straight up now and gets into fighting position. We're about ready to go another round when a blast of energy hits the ring. Roca looks up into the ring and his eyes go wide. I scan to where Roca is looking at, it's somewhere at top of the ring. I see a girl being held by a man, it takes me a second but I finally realize who it is. Its Sounni are old friend, Roca turns to look at me and says.

"They have her Shinruga". He puts his hand to his ear and pauses for a minute. Then his face goes grim.

"What did they say"? I ask.

"If I don't finish this soon and don't kill you, they'll slit her throat".

"Charge at me and lock fist". I tell him. He does when he gets up close to me, I explain to him we will fake my death. I back off, Roca makes a blast of enormous size. I jump to the wall of the arena, Roca fires off his blast. As it's coming at me I push the ring in as it's made of earth. I shield myself with energy and let the blast push me into the arena stadium. When the explosion goes off I disappear into the crowd. I can see the confusion coming from the crowd and the Roko gang people holding Sounni, are confused as well. I manage to get behind the one holding her and stab him in the head. The other members about to attack, when a blast of energy knocks him to the side. I look down and see Roca with his hand out and he nods, I nod back. Sounni's faints and is about to fall but I catch her. She looks up at me and says thank you. I nod and run back to the ring.

"Thank you Shinruga". Roca says.

"She's my friend too you know, nice work".

"Your idea". Roca says. "After this tournament I'm quitting the Roko gang".

"Good, you ready"? I ask.

"I had to use quite a bit of energy to make that explosion".He explains.

I nod my head and let out a blast of energy to make our power equal. He charges at me and punches with a force equal to boulder hitting the ground dropped from fifty feet. It takes both my hand to stop it, I slide backwards grinding against the ground. He comes at me once again I wait till the opportune moment and flip him over my shoulder. I raise my foot and try to kick him in the chest. He rolls away and turns firing off a blast. I charge up my hand and punch down and destroy the blast. I run at him throwing hits left and right. Clearly my martial arts skills are better, I charge up a blast of energy and hit him directly. Roca gets knocked down but gets back up even faster. Then sends a massive wave of earth at me. I catch and it sends me sliding back, Roca sends another one triple in size. I use some energy to destroy it. At the same time I throw out my hands and use the sparks from the friction and create lightning. I send it in Roca's direction, it destroys his earth attack. Roca tries to make a field of energy but he's too late. The explosion lets out to much smoke I can't see where Roca is. I'm on guard waiting for him to come out. I close my eyes to focus where he is, there he comes to my right and I block his attack. Knee him to the stomach, and roundhouse him to the face. I kick him but it turns to a snake, I blast its head off.

"Where are you"? I ask frantically searching out for his energy.

He comes out from behind me and block his first attack and some others but not all. I'm sent backwards and poise for battle again. I can see parts of Roca's body sparking, indicating where he was hit by my attack.

"Try this Shinruga". Roca yells in anger. He starts charging up a blast that starts eating the ground.

"It's converting what it disintegrates into energy". I get ready for his attack. When he fires the blast I clench my fist and increase the lightning around his leg. It makes him fall to one knee and the enormous blast misses me by inches. I'm about to charge up an attack but Roca's attack curves and is heading in my direction. I run drawing my sword and when I get close enough to Roca I put the blade as close to his face as possible. At the same time I put a sheet of earth behind me, and Roca stops his blast right behind it.

"It's over Roca I win". I say.

"How do you figure, that blast will break through your earth defense".

"If you do that I will move forward and you'll be dead". "Give up now". We pause for a moment and he considers what I say. I think about any other scenario that could happen.

"Drop the blast". I say. He looks away for a moment and then drops it, the explosion is huge. My eyes go wide and Roca smirks.

"That would have finished me for sure". I say in a whisper. He nods, the announcer comes in the ring and grabs my right hand and announces my victory. The crowd goes wild, tournament officials come to me and give me a chest full of chanks. Chanks is the money of our present time, mainly pieces of the old change before our world came to be. I walk off the stage, as I'm walking over to the tournament officials Sounni comes up to me.

"Thank you, so much…You should stop into Shiran again. It's been a while". She says.

"Maybe we'll see". She gives me a hug and goes to Roca. They walk over to me and Roca tells me that Ruji's blade is in his stuff and a note has been left for officials that if he loses or dies it's mine.

"Thanks". I say. He tells me it's only fair, I won the match.

I find a tournament official and tell him where Ruji's body is and what town to take it to. I go to where Roca slept that night and find the sword. Picking it up and looking at it, it brings back all my memories of Ruji. I sense Shokon out of the corner of my eye.

"I would like to go with you Shinruga". He says.

"That's fine". I say.

We walk out of the stadium together, it takes us all day of walking and when it comes close to dark we make camp. I set up my tent which only takes a few seconds. Psychians use their energy for everything, from getting something, to fixing something or setting something up. After I get done I notice Shokon has collected some rocks and is setting them all around us. I ask him what he's doing, he ignores me for a second. Then he puts his sword in the middle and it makes an energy field.

"The rocks have energy in them, keeps us safe". He says.

I nod and go collect some wood for a fire. When I come back we make the fire, and sit around it.

"How did you do that"? He asks.

"What"? I ask.

"The lightning, how did you make it hurt his leg again"? He asks.

"My father taught me a lot, one thing was lightning memorizes our energy. So we can control it even after it leaves are hand". I explain.

"He was a good friend wasn't he"?

"Yeah, I'd rather not talk about it". I say. He nods and goes to his tent. I go to mine as well and enjoy my sleep.

The next day we get up early, collect are stuff and start on our way to my town. It takes us about half a day to get there. When we do my father greets us.

"Welcome back home son". He says.

My father The Capturer the one who beat those who had the Elemenka gems. Once the strongest Psychian in the world, now just a dad. He has spiky hair and a couple of scars on his body one on his neck and one on his face.

"I saw the body". He says.

"Ruji, I tried and went to the town but he was already gon".

I try to finish my sentence but I can't. I'm about to cry but I hold up my head. Don't worry about my dad tells me, he simply tells me to go see Ruji's mother and tell her the news. I knock on the door when I get there. Mrs. Thean opens the door for me and ask me to come in.

"Hey, Mrs. Thean" I say.

"How many times have I told you to call me Keira"? She demands. "I saw that they brought a body a little bit ago, you know whose it is"? She ask. I can see the look on her face might be picking up what I know.

"Yes". I pause and she looks at me with persistence. "The body is Ruji's, I'm sorry. I checked for a sign of life, there wasn't anything".

She grabs my face and tells me, she knows that I tried everything. I try to hand her Ruji's sword but she tells me he would have wanted me to have it. I go to my house and run into my mother on the way. A worry wart, she always worried about me when I left for training or anywhere. My father had a lot of enemies, so she was worried one of them might attack me to get to him. It doesn't help that one kidnapped me though.

"Where you going mom"? I ask.

"Over to Keira's". She says. As I expected she gives me a big hug and says to go home and get some rest.

"Ruji's funeral is tomorrow you were his best friend". She says.

I do, when I get home I go straight to bed. Only to wake up from a nightmare, my parents come in and console me. The next day we all go to the funeral, they ask me to make a speech.

"It's too hard, all I can say is that he was a good friend and was a good person". Is all I say.

When I pass by Ruji's coffin, I drop my rose and say what I think should be said.

"See ya later my good friend, I'll see you one day". I walk away with my head down and head home.

CHAPTER 4

A NEW FRIEND

Waking up the next day I head into the middle of town to see what the people are selling. My father comes up to me, he tells me that one of the Elemenka gem holders have been spotted. He tells me it's in the next town. Club a small town where everybody goes by an old code. The town was attacked and it's my responsibility to capture the gem. I get the rest of the supplies I need and go. Lots of stuff from old earth were left behind, foods and drinks. Other stuff as well but the food and drinks is what we live on. We make our own stuff from the vegetation around as well. I say one last goodbye to my mom and dad and Ruji's mom and go on my way.

It's at least a one day, but in case I run into who I'm supposed to I don't want to waste any energy. I'm walking through the woods when I see a small pool of water. I take all my clothes off and get in, it's a little cold. Using my piece of flint I scrape it across my sword, with the spark that comes I make fire and heat the water up.

"Ah". I let out a sigh of relief and enjoy the hot water. Sitting there I fall asleep for a few minutes. A rustle behind me wakes me up. When I look back I notice someone has stolen my bag and swords. I look around and I see the thief take off left of me. I throw my clothes back on and take to the trees. I jump from branch to branch when I finally see the thief I charge up a blast of energy and fire. It hits a big branch it goes right in front of him. I pounce on him the second he stops.

When I turn him over I'm surprised to see who it is. It's Jet from the tournament the kid who was snooping.

"Shinruga, how you doing"? He says like nothing has happened.

I charge up an energy blast in my hand and put it close to his face.

"Thief's don't last long in this world". I tell him. "Explain".

He says he's sorry for what he's done, and that he just needed it for freedom. He tells me about the biggest town in our world is under siege. The Apocalypse Unit has taken it over, and when Psychian's come in they are enslaved.

"Operation Pokerian, that's what that meant". I say aloud.

Jet asks what I'm talking about and I tell him about Kita and all that I know. He then tells me that Kita was the one who fronted it all. That he is the leader of the Apocalypse Unit.

"I was a slave they beat me and killed my parents when I was too young to remember. They want me to get that sword and bring it back to them". He tells me.

"I have to send word to my father he will get a hold of the right people". I say. Putting my hand out I shoot a blast of energy and it explodes twice. In our world we have messengers who come when you signal them. We wait a half an hour and one comes. She hands me an ink pen and piece of paper. When I get done I tell her to go to Recnamorcen, and give the letter to Shinsaga Deshreneto. She goes, Jet and I start heading towards Club. When we get to Club the people of the town tell us that are Psychian has went towards Shiran. We start walking to Shiran, it takes us until late afternoon and were just a couple of miles out of Shiran. I yell out to Jet to jump a blade sweeps across the ground. When I and Jet land we look in the direction of where it came. There is a man whose blade is retracting.

"My name is Eurick and you must be Shinruga". He says. "Heard you're after me, and this".

Eurick is big and strong looking he's a little gangly looking as well. A white complexion and stringy hair. He shows me the gem inside the blade. I notice that he's twenty feet away and his blade was right by us. He has an extender blade, we must be careful.

"Jet you ready, he's going to kill us if we don't kill him". I tell him.

Jet nods his head and we wait, when Eurick makes a move we dodge him easily. He slices across to try to hit us both but we jump over it again. We charge at him shooting energy but he retracts his sword and just bats them away. We rain down energy onto Eurick but he starts spinning his blade and bats it away. Eurick is about to slash at Jet, and it takes me till now to notice that Jet doesn't have a blade of his own.

"Jet". I call out and throw him Ruji's blade.

The second Jet catches it he puts it up in defense. It knocks him back when he can stand still he summons a Phercon beast. I realize that this fourteen year old has some potential. It took Ruji four years to be able to do that. Eurick swings the blade at the beast but it's no good. When the beast gets close Eurick puts his blade away and locks fist with the Phercon.

"No way". Jet says.

Eurick throws the beast to the ground and stabs it. I'm almost to Eurick when he throws his blade up, I duck and slide on the ground. When I jump up Eurick shoots me with energy, Jet comes from behind and hits him with energy. He swings and slashes, Jet blocks. I send a piece of rock at Eurick but he kicks it. Jet and I get on each side of Eurick and fire blast at him, he puts both his hands out and stops them. The energy is starting to build up in his hands, Eurick jumps back. His evasion sends our blast of energy at each other. I catch it in time but Jet doesn't, he barely guards himself from the explosion. Jet is slammed against a tree and is knocked out cold. Eurick extends the sword his way, I throw a kunai and it makes Eurick's sword miss Jet by inches. I see a nearby puddle of water and splash it on Jet's face. It takes him a few seconds to wake up but when he does, he immediately sends a piece of earth hitting a tree and knocks it down. When Eurick is distracted I grab him from behind trying to strangle him. He grabs me by the ponytail and throws me to the ground. Jet jumps from the side and punches him in the face. I kick my right foot up with energy and hit him in the gut. Eurick spins releasing energy and knocks us both back. Before we can even think Eurick has his blade already extended and is striking at us. That's when I notice it the sunlight hitting his blade, I can see the energy in his blade. Strung out and weaker.

"Jet, get in closer I need his blade retracted". I tell him.

I throw my blade up and cutting the trees where Eurick is, so the sun will hit his blade. When we get closer he retracts his blade. The energy in the blade is close.

"Back off hurry". I yell. When we step back Eurick extends his blade again.

"What was that Shinruga to chicken to make a move"? He says with arrogance.

I get up close to Jet and tell him about what I noticed.

"You could break his sword if you hit it with enough force. Where's your blade"? He asks.

I nod where my blade has landed in the tree above Eurick. We both go in formation, shooting energy to keep him distracted. I jump up and grab the blade. While Jet keeps him busy I see where the blade is the weakest. I jump down and slash the blade at the point it is weakest. Eurick moves and retracts the blade back.

"I see what you're doing now, good eye you have there". He says.

"Now what"? Jet ask.

"We have to make him think that he has one of us. Make him extend his blade, so I can break it". I tell him. "We'll have to take a lot of damage just to convince him, you ready for that"?

"Yeah, let's do it".

"How cute let's hurry this up now". Eurick yells.

He fires off a few blast of energy, instead of staying back Eurick charges at us. Me and Jet scramble but remember that we need to stay close. We get hit by what he throws at us, my body can only stand so much before it will give up. Eurick hits me so hard that I fly backwards and can't get up for a few seconds. He pins Jet up against a tree using energy, and starts extending his blade to stab him.

"Ha, look at Shinruga Eurick". Jet lets out a little chuckle.

Eurick looks back and what he thought was me, is actually a earth statue of me that disintegrates. I make sure that Eurick has no time to think. I strike his blade at the precise point. The blade snaps in half with the broken half Eurick tries to stab me. I can't block the attack, the earth moves below me and I'm moved behind Eurick. I twist my body as fast as possible and plunge my sword deep into Eurick's back. Into his heart, when I look at Jet his hand is extended out. He was the one who moved me behind Eurick.

"How...It's not possible". Eurick mutters as his last words.

"You lost". I say.

Eurick falls over and I check his pulse. He's dead I tell Jet, and we take a minute to take a breather. Jet took most of the pain to ensure that we would win. I grab the piece of the blade that has the Elemenka gem. When I put the gem close to my sword it's absorbed into its slot on my handle. I can feel the immediate feel of evil coming from the gem but I shake it off. It's going to be a long walk to Shiran, considering I have to carry Jet all the way there. I can feel my arms getting heavy. Should I just leave Jet here and take Ruji's blade with me it's what I came for after all. I can't he helped me with the Elemenka gem but he did steel my stuff and the blade. No it wouldn't be right, I'll talk to him after we get some rest. We're still going when some guys jump down from the trees in front of us. There is three of them, strong looking Psychians. They are all scary looking, teeth rotten and black clothes. The one who is obviously the leader tells me that he wants my sword. I'm wondering what everybody wants this sword for. He tells me that he's going to take it and kill us both.

"You can try". I yell.

Even though I don't know what were going to do. Hoping that I think of something to get us out of here alive. I don't even have enough energy to block or make one attack. The three make a move, the leader is really close to me. My eyes are closed when the leader is really close to me, that's when a wolf made of energy comes out and tackles the leader. He recovers from the force of the blow and looks around for his opponent. The wolf is staring him and his comrades down. A man comes out from on top of a tree, when he lands and stands straight up I realize who it is. It's Furrock, my dad's best friend. Let him be or face death you three. The leader charges again and Furrock takes him on. His wolf intercepts the other one. The third one is coming at me, I grab my sword and wait for the right time. Right as he gets to me he swings his sword. I'm too slow and won't be able to block the attack. A blade goes in front of his to block the slash. I look up at my savior, it's Roca. I'm confused but I soon find out what's going on.

"Roca, hurry up my wolf won't last forever". Furrock yells hurriedly.

Roca starts hitting with such force it drives his opponent back. Furrock's wolf is struck with one of the three guy's sword and vanishes.

Furrock tells Roca to give me some energy. He does and I stand and fight but it doesn't last long. My opponent hits me with a huge blast of energy and I fall. He comes at me but Furrock gets in his way. He stabs my opponent and blocks the leaders attack as well. Roca blast the leader and dodges his own opponents attack. When the leader is knocked to the ground Furrock jumps on top of him. Using one his best attacks Furrock grabs the leader's throat. Using the force of a wolfs jaw squeezes his throat till he's dead. The third opponent stops when he sees this and runs. Roca comes up to me, he asks me if I'm ok. I try to talk but the blast that I was hit with has really drained me. It isn't too long until till I pass out.

"Shinruga, wake up, wake up".

I see Jet standing over me, shaking me telling me to get up.

"Where are me and what's going on, did we win, is Eurick dead"? He asks.

I get up and tell him what happened and tell him I have no idea where we are. Roca comes into the room and tells us to come into the living room.

We come into the living room and there is some food on a table for us. I look around the room and it seems familiar. The room is very neat with stuff from our time and from old earth as well. We eat and Sounni comes out of a room and then Furrock. He stands in front of me with a stern look on his face. He has a big scar on his right hand and I know where he got it from. I gave it to him when I was just a kid. I was messing with my sword, when it was my father's. Furrock tried to stop me and I accidentally cut him.

"Your father is on his way, my daughter is an excellent healer. You don't owe her nothing though, I heard about how you saved her at the tournament". His serious look goes to a smile. "I want to thank you personally". He says.

He goes on to tell me that the three who attacked me were from Pokera. Sounni asks us both if we want something to drink. We both say yes and she hands us some lemonade.

"What do they want with this blade, why is it so important"? I ask in aggravation.

He explains that the blade possibly has a Shard in it.

"It's very important to keep that blade with you, no matter what". He tells me.

There's more to the story of the Triple Psychian. When the Triple Psychian fought his opponent his sword was broken. The sword broke into twenty one pieces, they have all been forged into swords or other weapons as well. When the twenty pieces are brought back together the new Triple Psychian will emerge. Only twenty Shards have actually been used, the twenty first piece absorbs the energy a shard and then puts it back. It's a way of telling you your blade has a shard.

Furrock goes on to tell me that the twenty first shard is here in Shiran. My father is going to come to the city tomorrow to take me to school with the Shard. Furrock tells us that he has a spare bedroom that I and Jet can stay for the night. A couple of hours pass and I go outside where Roca is sitting.

"Who's the kid"? He asks.

"I'm not sure, don't think he does either. All he knows is his name is Jet".

I talk with him for a little bit and then I go into the house. Furrock is sitting at the kitchen table and ask me to sit down.

"Do you understand what I'm telling you Shinruga"? He asks me. "You have to hold that blade till your last dying breath, it cannot get into the wrong hands. Even though there is evil Psychians with that blade at the tournament it will be your job to stop them. A tainted Triple Psychian might destroy are already messed up world. Your father and I in our time helped keep this world safe. Especially your father he put his life on the line more times than I can count".

"I know and I will to". I tell him.

"Your father won't be as serious with you as I will. He always was a free spirit and a goof off, kind of envied that about him".

We talk for a little bit more and then I go into the area with books from old earth. Jet is in the room reading some books.

"Hey, man what's going on". He says.

"Nothing much, can I tell you something"? I ask.

He tells me sure and I explain to him I want him as a friend. I want to know if he is going to steal from me again.

"No, I almost died for your cause. I want to help you and help those in Pokera".

He goes on to tell me that he considers me as a brother. Even though we haven't spent much time together. We put our hands together, then pick up some books and start reading. Furrock asks us to come outside and help him hunt. We're in the woods for about twenty minutes, I see a deer. I jump from two trees and shoot energy at the stag. The energy misses, it tries to run Furrock's energy wolf tackles the beast. The wolf bites it throat, and vanishes Furrock shows up a few seconds later. He starts cleaning the deer, we all take it back home. Sounni and Roca clean the deer. Jet, Roca and I go back to the book room. I'm not sure what the book is about, from what I've read it's about a girl who has to find a stone.

"Jet, how is it that you were able to make a Phercon beast so fast"? I ask.

"I'm not sure. Instinct I guess, maybe this blade is just compatible with me". He says.

"Could be"?

"I'm sorry".

I tell him it's okay and go back to reading my book.Sounni comes into the room and tells us that it's time for lunch. I catch Sounni looking at me out of the corner of her eye. I look when she isn't looking, she's the most beautiful women I've ever seen. From what I hear she looks almost like her mother. Blonde hair, perfectly proportioned body and the voice of an angel. When it's close to night around nine thirty I and Jet say we're going to turn in. Sounni shows us to our room and we unpack our stuff. I notice Jet is messing with something in his bag, when I ask him what it is he tells me it's nothing and hides it. We turn in for the night and for once it's not full of nightmares.

CHAPTER 5

SIGN UP

My father arrives about nine o' clock the next morning. He walks in like it's his house. I introduce him to Jet and they shake hands. My father looks at him a little funny and just looks over to Furrock. He sits down in the living room talking everything over. Compliments Furrock on how the place looks. I've never seen my father look so patient. Seems like Furrock has something to do with his new state of mind.

"I had no idea the blade had a Shard in it son". He says.

I can tell he didn't know that the sword had the Shard. He tells me he also got the letter that I sent him. Furrock ask my dad what the letter was about. My father points at Jet and ask if he would tell Furrock what it was about.

"It's about the city of Pokera, it's under siege by the Apocalypse Unit". He says.

"That's a shame, it's one of our biggest cities. Shinsaga, did you mail a letter to Hiraski"? Furrock asks.

I hear a glass drop to the ground. It was Sounni, she lets out a gasp. Furrock asks her what's wrong.

"Rikki". She says.

Furrock tells us about his cousin who went to Pokera a couple of years ago. They haven't heard anything from him in a while. I feel bad for them, and even worse because this would be second time they've lost someone. It was ten years ago tomorrow come to think of it. Twelve years ago my family and Furrock's lived in Shiran. It was a Thursday morning, I was woken up by bombs. I went outside to watch but my dad pushed me back inside. The AU (Apocalypse Unit) attacked and my father and Furrock fought them off Sounni's house was one of the first to be attacked. She lost her mother that day. Furrock fought as hard as he could and so did my dad. It took until three in the afternoon to kill them all. When it was all said and done the town was reduced to practically rubble. Furrock never forgot that day, he hasn't been the same since that day. Twenty three people dead and no homes for the survivors. My father packed up what little stuff that we had, and moved to Renamorcen. Which at that time was nothing but people flocked to the city to be under my dad's watchful eye.

It's noon now and my father tells me we should head to the school. I'm really nervous and my father can see that. He puts his arm around me and tells me not to worry. When we get there, there is a whole bunch of young Psychian's. Trying to sign up for classes I suppose. Furrock walks up to a young but still older Psychian, than the rest. It takes me a second to realize that this Psychian is the master. His name is Ikeya, he has a pair of small glasses. A formal uniform and a weird symbol on it. I can see by his uniform that he is a very tidy person. He takes us to a back room, when he turns on the light I can see it. The twenty first Shard of the Triple Psychian.

"When I ask you pull your blade out. The energy in your blade will go from yours to this one and back to your blade again. If it does, I will accept you into my school immediately". He says.

I notice that Jet is kind of hiding in the back for some reason, but I ignore the weird behavior.

"Classes start in two days you have till then to bring your stuff".

"My friend Jet would also like to join your school". I tell him.

"Well the friend of Shinruga, why not". He says. "See you in two days, be prepared for some intense training". He says.

Ikeya nods and goes into a different room. I tell Furrock to tell me everything he knows about Ikeya. He tells me that Ikeya is one the six royals. A royal in our world is someone who has completed a mission and done many things to help our kind. They're family is also one of the six who came up with our way of life. Who also showed us how to rebuild our world.

We leave the school, my father asks me if I want to go into town and look at some stuff for sale. Furrock takes Jet back to his house. My father goes into the market, he's like a kid picking everything up and looking at everything he possibly can. He picks up a pair of fighting boots and hands them to me.

"What's special about these"? I ask.

He tells me that they're Rock boots. When you're about to get hit if you add energy to them it puts a shield around your feet. I buy the boots and they actually look quite dashing on me. We enjoy the rest of the day shopping and looking for stuff. I buy a very nice looking necklace for my mom and tell my dad to give it to her. I also pick up something for Sounni. My dad ask who it's for and I tell him that I'm going to ask Sounni out for a date. The necklace is encased in silver and has a stone on it that has an emerald color to it, on the back of the silver part it has writing that says "Kryptonite". My father goes to the end of the town and tells me he has to get back home. He tells me good luck and gives me a small hug.

"Love you my son". He whispers.

Just like that he's gone, and I miss him already. I walk back to Furrock's and come inside, Furrock is at the kitchen table. Eating some food, Sounni is in the living room reading a book. I ask where Jet is at, Furrock tells me he's outside doing something to his new blade. I rush outside to see what he is doing to the blade.

"What are you doing to the blade"? I asks.

He holds the blade up to me and shows me a part of the blade. I examine the blade and see a part of it has a knick in it. Whoever forged this blade wasn't that good. The Phercon in the blade could have escaped. The last time that happened the Phercon was twenty times stronger than when it was put in there.

Furrock comes outside a few seconds later. He asks us what we're doing we tell him.

"Do you two want to spar with me"? He asks.

"Sure". I say.

I and Jet stand in ready for him. Furrock is calm and cool, he looks at us both with a conceited look on his face. He starts building up some energy, but Jet and I know what he's about to do. He's trying to summon and energy wolf. Jet acts quickly and slaps the ground and makes a piece of earth fly up at Furrock's ball of energy. Furrock's ball of energy disappears, he jumps over to us striking us with hard and fast blows. Jet manages to block a few but I'm not so lucky. It takes me a second to get up but Jet is able to hold his own for a little bit. When Jet falls from Furrock's barrage of attacks, I pick up right away. I shoot out a couple of energy blast at Furrock. He dodges one and cups another one in his hands, spins and fires it back.

"How did he do that"? I ask.

Furrock is vicious he's not like my father. He is straight to the point and accurate with his attacks. I have to wonder how my father ever beat him. After a few more minutes of sparring Furrock says that he has some business to attend to. Jet and I go back into the house and see that Sounni is still in the living room reading. She looks up for only a second and then goes back to reading. I ask Jet how he was able to block so many of Furrock's attacks.

"I don't know, I guess being imprisoned at Pokera made my reflexes above average". He says.

I nod and go to our room and wait for Furrock to return. I'm meditating when I hear a noise in the kitchen. I walk into the hallway, I look in the living room and I see Sounni holding a fireplace poker out. There is a man standing in the living room. His chuckle tells me of what his intentions are.

"Jet get out here now, leave now ". I yell at him.

"Furrock should have taught you to mind your own business". The man says.

"She is my business". I say.

"Nectoris is the name". He says.

He goes on to tell me that he was the one who targeted the city ten years ago. Jet comes out of the bathroom, he immediately senses the man and is on guard. How he got into the house I don't know the house door was never opened. I would've heard it open, so how did he get in. All the windows are closed. Jet is about to make a move I can see it. If this guy gets Sounni we're at a stale mate. I can see Jet getting more and more anxious but before he makes a move. That would otherwise put Sounni in harm's way, I think of something.

"Sounni, could you tell me if you know where your father keeps a set of kunai"? I asks.

She looks to the right of her and so does her opponent. When he does I throw one of my own kunai and it hits Sounni's weapon. Her weapon bounces off the wall behind her and stabs Nectoris in his arm. Knowing that fighting with one arm would be hard for him he bolts out the window. Glass goes flying out everywhere I push it with energy towards Nectoris. The glass misses him and Jet and I follow him. I jump in front of Nectoris to cut him off.

"You think we're going to just let you go I don't think so". I yell.

Nectoris is about to head to his right, but Furrock is there. I'm guessing he sees that the fire poker in Nectoris's arm is his.

"There you are Furrock. You going to fight me to kind of unfair don't you think"? He asks.

"Unfair would be fighting a little girl like you do". Furrock says.

Nectoris pulls the fire poker out of his arm and throws it at Furrock. It misses by a long shot of course.

"Nectoris I won't fight you frankly it would be too easy, these two will though". He says.

"Well then come on, let's see what you got". Nectoris says with a bead of sweat going down his face.

Jet charges as fast as he can. He attacks with such a ferocity I'm almost too stunned to move. Something he probably picked up from being in Pokera, don't stop attacking till you have no energy left. I finally start after Nectoris and fire a bunch of energy blast. Jet has him so distracted that he doesn't even see them. He's hit one after another, they hit him so hard he falls to the ground. Jet is over top of him ready to stab him, but Furrock stops him.

"I want him alive Jet". He yells.

We drag him back to Furrock's house and tie him up to a chair. It's hard to keep a Psychian held hostage because their hands can use energy. We use what's called a Hand Tazer. Every time the user uses energy it zaps them. He keeps asking what Furrock wants, but Furrock doesn't seem to mind him at all. Soon a mail person comes to the door and Furrock hands him a paper. Furrock tells Nectoris that he is going to stay there for a couple of days.

"What do you want"? He asks.

Furrock tells him that he will find out in a day or two. Also that he would be stupid to try to escape. With three Psychian's to hold him from escaping.

"Plus not to mention my daughter and a fire poker". Furrock says with a chuckle.

Nectoris lets out a little chuckle and as Furrock is in front of him, opens his mouth and lets out a mouthful of energy. Furrock barely evades the blast and punches him across the face. I think he punched him because it destroyed half of his kitchen.

"Hook a hand tazer to his mouth as well Shinruga". He says.

We wait and about four hours later a group of men come to Furrock's door. There is four of them, they are all in white and have a weird symbol on their uniform. When they walk in one of them talks to Furrock for a little bit. They untie Nectoris and walk him outside. I remember the look in Nectoris's eyes, it alarmed me down to the bone.

"Who are those guys Furrock"? I ask.

He just nods, goes outside and starts cutting down some trees. Sounni tells me that he is collecting some wood to fix the house. I get up go outside and start carrying in the wood. Jet starts cutting it into a certain length for the missing pieces of the house. Something he probably learned from fixing and building stuff at Pokera. Furrock comes in sees Jet and gives a smile of approval. He notices that I'm not doing anything, he tells me to cut a perfect square right down to the ground. Furrock gives Jet a bag of nails, he starts putting the wall together. It only takes us twenty minutes to put the whole wall together. Furrock uses his energy in the wall. Psychian's put energy in their walls so in case they are attacked from the outside, the energy will defend the house. Finding some sheet metal lying around the wall is put together in an hour.

"Good work you two". Furrock says.

We go back to the living room and start reading books. A couple of minutes later ask Furrock if I could use the shower.

"Sure, Jet and I need to go to town, to pick up some stuff for dinner". He says.

Jet nods and they go out the door. Going into the bathroom there is the toilet and the shower. To start a shower in our time there is a place below the pipe that you add some fire to. Using your energy you pull water from a lake. Which the pipes lead to, when the water passes through where the fire is it warms the water. It takes a few minutes to pull the water from the lake. It also takes a few minutes for the water to warm up. The shower is warm and soothing, considering what's happened to us all in the last few days. The door opens softly and I can see the figure of Sounni outside the curtain. She tells me there is a towel on the back of the toilet. I spend some amount of time in the shower, it's one of my favorite things to do. I get out and get dressed. Walking out Sounni ask if I can help her out. She needs help with the shower, Sounni is not Psychian so she can't work the shower. Normally Furrock has it set up so Sounni doesn't need his help.

"He does something with that knob down there but I never pay attention". She says.

I have to keep feeding the water or else she won't be able to take a shower. The curtain shows Sounni's outline as she's undressing.

"Shinruga". She yells.

Thinking that she's seen me looking at her outline in the curtain, I about fall off the toilet.

"Where is the water"? She asks.

"Oh, right. Sorry about that". I say.

The waters already pretty warm from the last time. When she's done I hand her the second towel on the back of the toilet. She steps out of the shower with the towel covering her breasts and private area. She gives me a funny look, it takes me a few minutes to understand what she wants. I go out of the bathroom and into the living room. Sounni comes out in a low cut white halter top and some black slacks.

"You look nice". I tell her.

She says thank you and goes to do the few dishes that are there.

We wait for Furrock and Jet to come back from their day of shopping. When they do get back Sounni and I mention nothing about us being in the bathroom together. They brought back some meat from the market and Furrock puts it in the freezer. Psychian's can manipulate any element, by using old freezers we make a block of ice and freeze everything. I've wanted to ask Sounni out to dinner since I met her, this last time especially. I notice that Furrock is in quite a good mood. While mopping the floor Sounni looks up to notice me looking at her.

"Sounni would you like to go to dinner sometime"? I ask.

Furrock's eyes dart to mine, then to Sounni's. I'm about ready to say it's all a joke.

"Sure, when and where"? She says excitedly.

Furrock is about to stand up but Sounni walks over to him. They whisper, when they're done Furrock stands up walks over to me.

"Take care of her and be good". He says.

After that Sounni walks over to me and tells me that we'll go to a place called Bickery's. First though she wants to go to town and look around before we go.

"What time"? I ask.

"Seven thirty". She says.

It's about four o' clock; she wants to go about five. I go to my room and spend time, getting ready for our date. I'm a little excited I must admit. Noticing Furrock's reflection in the mirror, I tell him he can come in.

"That is my daughter, hurt her…Well you're just lucky Shinsaga is my best friend". He says. "Have fun on your date. I'm glad though it's you, couldn't ask for anyone else than the son of my own best friend". He says.

It's about four thirty. We're all sitting in the living room. Sounni comes out in an all red dress thatgoes just above her knees. Her hair is completely straightened but the top is put into a rubber band in the back. I like this look it makes her look so beautiful. My eyes go wide but I catch it in time to look natural.

"You look nice Shinruga". She says.

I'm dressed in a white button down, nice looking slacks and some dress shoes.

"It complements the red in your dress". I blurt out.

She giggles a little and grabs me by the arm and drags me out the door practically. Furrock stops us right as we're about to get out the door, puts out his arm for a hug from Sounni. She gives him a hug tells Furrock that she'll be all right and we go.

We're just at the edge of the city; Sounni sees some shoes that she thinks would go perfectly with her dress. The shop owner tells me that they're a few chanks, so I hand them to him. She immediately puts them on, she lights up in satisfaction. We walk through the city till we get to the restaurant called Bickery's. We get into Bickery's and it's filled with people eating, the food looks spectacular. I can tell it's a formal restaurant. The lady who works at the restaurant comes over to us. She tells us that the special for the day is steak and potatoes. She asks us what we would like to drink. I order us both a glass of white wine and some water.

"Shinruga, why did you want to go out with me"? She asks.

My emotions start to talk for me, I start saying random things.

"I get it". She says.

We enjoy the rest of our dinner, pay for it and leave. Going down the street there is everything from demonstrations of different attacks, people dancing to music. A slow song comes on when we are going by the other people. Sounni grabs my hand, pulling me back to her. Placing my hand in hers and the other on my shoulder. The man in the song is singing about never letting go of someone. We get lost in each other's arms, Sounni gets closer and closes her eyes. We dance till that song is over, never letting go of each other through the whole song. Walking down the street we see a light, as we get closer it moves further back. Immediately I sense them, two figures from the right. Pushing Sounni back I'm able to dodge the two men's energy blast.

"My name is Dart". The man says.

I tell him I could care less, and ask him what his intentions are. He smiles and tries to attack but I just knock him down. They aren't that strong but two on one are never good odds.

"You're the kind of scum that sneaks up on a person, knocks them out and steals their stuff". I say.

Those kinds of people make me sick. The ones who can't even fight like a real man. With honor the main moral of a Psychian.

Dart comes at me once again, I knock him down again. Making sure that the other guy doesn't sneak up on me or Sounni either. Two city guards come over they both charge up some energy. Realizing who I am they point their hands at Dart and his friend. They ask us who they are and what they wanted with us.

"Just a couple of thugs". I say.

Sounni grabs my arm again. She is trembling I can feel it. We go to a place by a lake, Sounni sits down by a big tree. Sitting beside her she tells me about when the city was attacked ten years ago and how she misses her mother. I grab her around her arms and we sit there. We accidentally fall asleep under the tree. When I wake the sun is bright in my eyes, Sounni is laying in my arms still. I shake her, when she wakes up, she lets out a gasp.

"Dad". She yells. "He's going to kill us both".

We run back to her house, when we get inside Furrock is sitting at the table tapping his fingers. He points his finger to the chair, he wants me to sit.

"Baby girl go into your bathroom the shower is ready for you". He says with a killer look on his face.

I sit in the chair he's pointed to, Furrock says nothing at first.

"...Shinruga, that's my little girl if anything happened". He starts to say.

"The truth is nothing happened, we sat under a tree and accidentally fell asleep". I say.

He gives and a sigh, I ask him what's wrong. Furrock puts his hand on a mirror, he gets the image in his head. Adds some energy to the mirror, I get up to look. The image that he has on the mirror is of a picture of him and his wife. They're under the same tree that Sounni and I slept under.

"I and Sounni's mother stayed under that same tree, it's one of the only things in town that wasn't destroyed ten years ago". He says. "Sounni will go to that tree every year on the day her mother died, she misses her so much".

"I see".

Furrock tells me that I can go. I stay instead asking Furrock many questions about Sounni's mother and the attack on Shiran.

It's not too long until Sounni comes out. She asks me if I want to go into town again.

"Daddy is it all right"? She asks.

"Yeah, sure". He says.

We get into town and the city streets are bustling with people. The hours go by quickly while we're together. Furrock greets us when we get back to his house, food is strung out along the table.

"I've been through all the forms of training. The food is not the greatest. So for your last meal here I've prepared a big dinner for all of us".

The dinner is fabulous Furrock tells me that Sounni's mother came up with all the recipes.

When everyone is done with dinner, Sounni brings out all the deserts. When the dishes are done we all go into the living room and watch a movie. Something about people skipping some holiday of old earth.

Psychian's can use their power to repair or make any electrical device work again. When the movie is over we go to the school. When we're about to go in to the school Sounni grabs my head and kisses me like she never has.

"See you when you get out". She says.

I nod and Jet and I go into the school. Into our room and unpack a lot of our stuff, we both drop onto our beds and turn in.

"Night Shinruga, tomorrow we start our classes". He says.

"Did you even go to classes to get your Shogun training"? I ask.

He tells me that it was something he worked on when he could.

"Good to know". I say.

I turn over and drift off to sleep, waiting for the morning. Some Psychian's despise me, because of my father. I met someone in my training who wanted me dead, my father killed his father. Since that day he vowed revenge.

My teacher Sochajo watched out for me, when he tried to kill me Sochajo stopped him. Since that day he left me alone.

I lie there waiting for the nightmares to come but they never do.

Chapter 6

Kimoshiran Training Starts

A bell rings for us students to wake up. We get out to the training center, all the students are lined up we follow their lead. I can see many Psychian's standing around, the training center is double the size of my teachers in Recnamorcen. Ikeya is walking up and down the rows of students. His usual demeanor has changed his eyes are intense.

"For any of you who think my class will be easy quit now". He says.

He glares at the students to see any weakness in their face.

"Can any of you students tell me who the first Kimoshiran was"? He asks. None of the students raise their hand. "The first Kimoshiran was Shingo lee, he came up with the name and was the first to use Kimo the energy. He is also responsible for finding out about the humans who started the Great War. Today you will learn what a Kimoshiran is capable of and what sets them aside from the other two kinds. A Kimoshiran is able to put out double the power of energy, the damage that you can do is double of the other forms. Kimoshiran's can also see weak points in his enemy's body".

Ikeya goes on talking for the rest of the class, which last about another hour. Ikeya tells us that tomorrow he will show us how to get into Kimoshiran form.

To change into the other forms you have to say the chant for that form of Psychian. You only have to say the chant once. After that use the right hand sign and you will change into the form anytime.

That's what sets us apart from the Triple Psychian. Something about his dna allowed him to accomplish this, it's said that when you win the tournament, your sword absorbs the last bit of energy the dna of the Triple Psychian combines with yours. This is what will allow us to become the Triple Psychian. No one knows how he was able to use all three energies at once. The combination of all three energies at once creates an unimaginable power. He was a ghost who came out of nowhere and destroyed what was called the government of new. There is no record of what he looked like, no ancestors to ask about him.

After class Jet and I go into our room. We spar a little and wait for the bell to ring for lunch in the cafeteria. We go into the cafeteria and half of the Psychian's are staring at us. After we get our food, Jet and I sit down by ourselves. It doesn't take long before two Psychian's sit down beside us. Something catches Jet's eyes, I follow to see what he's looking at. It's a girl, she looks to be about Jet's age and she's now staring at Jet and I.

"You're Shinruga right". She asks.

I'm not surprised when this Psychian girl asks this. I'm pretty use to this by now, people coming up to me and asking if I'm Shinruga.

"If you know why are you asking"?

She just shrugs her shoulders and goes back to eating. I can tell she knew but just wanted to talk to me. She's pretty long brown hair down to her shoulder, button nose, high cheek bones and hazel eyes that are almost gray.

"Well aren't you going to tell us your names or just sit there stuffing your faces in front of us"? I ask.

The girl puts down her fork; she tells us that her name is Sorona.

"Is that your boyfriend"? I ask.

Their facial expression looks as though if they're about ready to puke.

"No, ewe, this is my brother Sange".

I ask them where they are from. Sorona tells me that they were born and raised in Shiran. Sange and Sorona go on talking to their selves here and there. Jet asks Sorona the occasional question. I listen but don't really pay attention to any of them. My ears pick up the name Sounni.

"Sounni, Furrock's daughter"? I ask.

"Yes, she's my best friend; she told me she was going steady with someone".

"I would be the person she's going steady with".

I ask Sange and Sorona what type of Psychian they were when they born. They were both born Psychian warrior. It's the reason they haven't done their Kimoshiran training already.

When Psychian's are born they start out as one of the forms of Psychian's. When they are ready most go to a school to perfect their skills. After that they can choose to go for the other two classes of Psychian or stay as they are.

As we're eating I feel an ominous energy, looking behind me there is a Psychian walking by me. Sorona tells me not to look directly at him, his name is X.

"X's, family was killed off when he was a baby. I've heard from people that your father might have been responsible for their demise". She tells me. "From what I hear though they were evil and so your father had no choice".

I'm done eating my food now, but the only thing I have on my mind is X. How could my father kill off a whole town?

"Does anybody know what the name of the town is"? I ask.

Sorona just shakes her head no. Her face goes wide with fear; I sense the blast just in time. Jumping to the side I can see my attacker. It's X holding his hand out and fresh with energy.

"You don't have the right to speak about my family". X's face is angered.

"It's just a rumor; we don't know if that's what happened". I say.

"Maybe since the girl said it I should blast her instead". He says.

Jet jumps up the second X says his remark.

"Blast her and you'll deal with me". He says.

X fires another blast but it is stopped by another. Ikeya is standing in the doorway of the cafeteria with his hand out.

"There will be no fighting unless you are outside or in the training room". Ikeya yells for all the students to hear.

We go on about the rest of the day in our rooms waiting for the next day to come. Ikeya is going to show us how to change into the Kimoshiran form. A knock comes at my door, I go to see who it is. When I open the door, X is standing on the other side of the hall. X is wearing a black trench coat, I noticed before he has a weird shaped x on the back. His hair is a little messed up, his eyes are almost completely gray.

"I don't know if your father killed my family or not but best not to talk about it if I were you". He says.

"Don't lose yourself X, you have a lot of power. You can help". I say.

My shard on my sword starts lighting up. This means mine and X's shards were right next to each other on the Triple Psychian's sword.

X notices his blade also lighting up, after that he leaves.

"Looks like we might have to fight another time". Thinking to myself.

For some reason the shards won't transfer their power until the day of the tournament. Even if two people who have shards fight before that time. I go back to my room and see Jet sitting there on his bed. I ask him where he's been all day. He tells me he's been training all day with Sange and some of the other students.

"I think I'm one of the strongest here". He says.

Personally I think X and I are the strongest but I could be wrong. I'm a little arrogant; get it from my dad I guess he was always like that when he was younger. He grew out of it but he's still arrogant around Furrock. That's just to bug Furrock though, it gets to him so easily.

Sorona comes to our door, asking how Sounni and I met. I asked if she knew that Furrock and my father were friends. She tells me that she vaguely remembers. If she doesn't know I'm not surprised. After the incident happened in Shiran, my father and mother hardly came back there.

"I saw X coming from this direction did he come see you"? She asks.

I tell her what he said to me and how I should just avoid him. She nods and thinks that would be best. Sorona leaves the room, Jet and I keep our selves busy for the rest of the night.

The next day the bell rings and we go to class. Ikeya tells the students to get into formation.

"Students today I will teach you the phrase and hand sign to get into Kimoshiran form". He tells us.

"Ready here is the hand sign the phrase to speak is Cambiar".

Half the students get it on the first try, even Jet gets it right. It takes me a few tries to get it right, the space around me lights up in color blue. The azure blue energy is circling around me and when it's done. My appearance has not changed, but when some energy comes into my hand it's blue. My sword has been replaced with my Kimoshiran blade the monkey blade. My father picked it up for me when I was a kid and saved for when I was going into my Kimoshiran schooling.

"Now at first you won't be able to stay in this form for long about two hours, some less some more". He tells us. "Be ready for some intense pressure on your body. When you change into this form double the output means double the energy in your system as well".

Just as he says this I hit the ground, looking around half the students are on their knees as well. It takes about an hour. I'm feeling too weak I have to change back into Psychian warrior.

"Amoeba".I say.

The purple energy goes all around me and I feel like I'm back to myself again.

"Change into this form often and train hard. Release energy it will help take off some of the pressure till you get use to it". He informs us. "Class over".

When I leave I go back to the room for just a second to put some stuff in my pocket away. I feel something evil though, to the point where my stomach is throbbing. I ignore the pain and walk down the hallway. Hoping to find Jet, Sorona or Sange I instead run into X.

"Saw you in class, couldn't handle the pain"? He asks me.

Now that I think back to it, X didn't even look like he was in pain. He tells me he realizes why are blades were lighting up.

"If you keep this up you won't stand a chance in the tournament, it's for the strongest fighters and you're too weak I can tell". He tells me.

X's face almost scares me half to death, I don't understand why it matters to X. If beating me will be so easy, why do I threaten X so much?

Walking outside there is a crowd of Psychian's around Sorona, my first thought is that she is in a fight.

I run over to see but instead of seeing her fighting, she's standing there alone and everyone is cheering her on.

"Shinruga, Sorona is the fastest at sword racing. She's beaten everyone here". Jet tells me. "For a girl she's not too bad".

It takes a Jet a second to realize what he just said, he turns slowly to see that Sorona. Whose face has took on almost a demon like appearance.

"For a girl she's not too bad". She yells.

She lifts up her leg and Jet goes flying he hits the ground hard. He brings his head up, spinning dazed from the kick and fall.

"Didn't I mean anything by it"? Jet says in gibberish.

"You probably gave him brain damage from that sis". Sange says.

Sorona and Sange argue for a few seconds. As I'm about to leave Sorona calls my name out.

"Hey, don't think you're going to get away that easily". Sorona warns.

I turn around to see that Sorona put her sword down on the ground. I know all too well what she's asking for, a sword racing match.

"Come on Shinruga one lap, it's always said that Shinsaga's prodigal son will surpass his own father one day".

I can't argue with her on that note, it's what I've been hearing all my life. The son of Shinsaga will be twenty times his own father's strength.

"All right fine, I'll verse you". I say.

Sorona and I get are blades ready for riding. Sange puts out his hand making a ball of energy, he shoots the blast. The blast makes a path that will be the race track.

"When I beat you don't be surprised". Sorona hollers.

The crowd behind us is going wild as we wait for Sange to start the race. His hand goes down, we're off. Sorona is already a hundred feet away or so ahead. I start blasting at her to slow her down, she dodges all of my attacks. Distracted she's going to fast though and almost hits a tree. This is my time to catch up, I use more energy. She and I are now head to head, but not for long. Sorona is blasting at me but misses with all of her blasts. Sorona turns up the juice and is once again far from me. We come to a part of the track where the wind is now against us, even Sorona is struggling. I'm struggling even more now, with the finish line in sight. An idea sparks I use my energy to create a tunnel to block the wind. My plan worked and I'm going faster than ever, I pass Sorona. She soon catches on and does as I do. She is catching up again,

I think quickly. I use my energy to hit the ground a couple of yards in front of her.

"Are you kidding me that was the worst aim ever"? She yells.

The ground in front of her comes up. At first she thinks I have made an obstacle in front of her and is about to avoid it, when she sees that it is smooth. Sorona smiles and hits the ramp, when she does I use my energy to make her go higher up into the air. I put more energy into my sword to go faster, Sorona finally lands a few feet behind me. She's too late I've already cleared the finish line.

"How did you win, what was the point of the ramp"? She asks.

"I made the ramp to keep you up in the air longer to slow you down. You lost Sorona". I say.

The crowd goes nuts chanting my name, Shinruga the fastest Psychian. Even though I know this is not true, I don't feel like saying it. I feel the presence of eyes on me, instead of it being X it's someone else. His long brown hair and his Shogun patch on his left arm. He turns and goes towards the school. I notice that when he turns around there is another symbol on his back. It looks almost like four triangles and a circle in the middle. Each of the triangles is the different colors of the Psychian energies. The middle of the symbol is white.

"Jet, do you know who that is"? I ask him.

"No…Never seen him before, he was staring at you though".

I nod my head and continue to walk, I go into the school. The Shogun with the brown hair comes from around the corner.

"Shinruga my name is Yamasaki". He introduces.

I nod and try to walk away again but he stops me.

"I just want to warn you to stay away from Ikeya, he's not to be trusted. My informants have reason to believe he is part of the Apocalypse unit".

"What does that matter to me"? I ask.

He goes on to tell me that Ikeya is trying to persuade Psychian's with shards in their blades.

"Be safe and watch yourself Shinruga you could be the fate of the Psychian race as we know it". He explains.

I go back to my room and sit on the bed, cup my hands together and start asking myself, how could I be the one Psychian who could save our people? Why did I have to be one who got a blade with a shard. I lay down and drift off to sleep to wait for my next day to come.

CHAPTER 7

SPARRING GOES WRONG

The scheduled bell sounds the next day I get out of bed sore, but ready for class. Sorona, Sange and Jet are all waiting for me. I tell them about what Yamasaki said to me.

"How weird"? Sorona says.

The students file into the class Ikeya is standing in the middle of the room. He tells us students to sit on the floor.

"By now you should be able to stay in the Kimoshiran form for a couple of hours now". He tells us. "One of my own moves that I teach to my students, and one of the most dangerous ones. Only use this move if you think you are completely ready. If you mess this up you will be sent to a place underground full of cannibals and monstrous creatures".

Half of the students wander their eyes in amazement, whispering to each other. Wondering if such a place could exist. One of the students raise their hand, she ask master Ikeya if he's just trying to scare us or if it exist.

"I personally know about this place. My friend Krautz messed it up; he escaped and lives here in Shiran". He tells us.

Ikeya puts his hands in a certain formation. Putting his fingers towards the ground and making his hands form the shape of a circle. A red circular portal being black in the middle shows up under Ikeya's feet. The students point, some warn Ikeya. Ikeya smiles and the portal starts sucking him in. In an instant Ikeya is gone and so is the portal. All the students are wondering where are master has disappeared to.

"Behind you". Master Ikeya says.

When I look back Ikeya is standing behind all the students. More whispers from the students, dumbfounded by are master's appearance. Ikeya walks through the middle of all the students.

"I call it the Kimoshiran Gateway". He says. "I use it very little because it takes a lot of energy and it's just too dangerous for my liking".

Ikeya points at X and I.

"X, Shinruga. You two fight". Ikeya says.

The crowd falls silent; their faces tell what they are thinking. A long awaited battle and rivalry, X couldn't be happier. I can see that smirk on his face. To inflict pain on me, his satisfactory will be achieved.

"About time I've been waiting for this moment". X says.

"If you want to fight that bad then I won't take it easy on you". I say.

"To bad it won't be a fair fight".

Ikeya comes in between us and tells us the extent of power we can use. He also tells us to fight fair, he raises his hand. We prepare getting into our fighting poses.

"Fight". Ikeya yells.

X is right in front of me in a flash, I'm barely able to block his attack. X steps back just long enough for me to charge up some energy. I send the blast at him, but he cuts it in half with his sword. I'm about to back up but there is a wall of energy behind me. I look to Ikeya who's one hand is feeding energy to the wall.

"You have to learn to fight in small places Shinruga". Ikeya tells me.

Before I can say anything to Ikeya, X is ready to strike me. I duck and his fist hits the wall of energy. I trip him, filling my hand with energy and striking down at my opponent. He easily avoids by rolling forward. I run after him, he starts firing blast while on one knee. I unsheathe my sword slashing at the blast of energy. I slash once more to finish him off, but he jumps backwards still firing. X's accuracy is incredible hitting me with all of his aerial blasts. My breath has been taken away, but I have to get up so that I will not be beaten.

"This is all that you can offer me Shinruga, I thought you would at least last for more than a few seconds". X says.

With my right hand I fire a blast completely missing X. It distracts X just long enough to tackle him to the ground. Several of my punches meet his face but it's not too long before he uses one of his hands to twist my arm and knock me off of him. He lands a roundhouse kick loaded with energy, that about knocks me out. Recovering as quick as possible I look for X, it's as if he's disappeared. That's when the sound of X's foot alarms me. He's behind me, his blade coming down. I throw mine up to defend, the force drives me to one knee.

"Come on Shinruga, fight better. You're taking it easy". X says in anger.

He's just like Roca so angry but still able to think clearly while in the middle of a fight. It's time for me to power up. The energy starts to flow from my body, the dark purple energy starts to increase.

About time you're using your full power". X says.

I don't give X a second to think, my right fist strikes his cheek with a force that knocks him into the energy wall. X takes no time to recover as he's already up and exchanging blows with me. His strength increases with every attack even when he's taking damage. X backs off for a few seconds just long enough to create a tonfa out of energy. Both his hands have become dangerous weapons with his strength increasing still. X charges wielding his weapons of death. X strikes with his blade first but is surprised when I block his tonfa.

"Your sheathe".

"Lined with steel and energy so it's harder to break". I explain.

X and I go head to head but are energies are starting to decrease. My sheathe stands no chance against X's blade, cutting it in half. I strike his tonfa making it disappear, at the same time X's blade is nearly to my throat. Thinking quickly I add energy to the energy boots my dad got me. I flip backwards with the shield on my feet. The shield blocks X's attack, sending his blade flying out of his hands. I fire an energy blast to stun X, it doesn't work. He merely swats it away and punches the ground. Sending energy and earth at me, I put up a shield of energy. Half of the explosion hits me knocking me to the ground. I hold the area where my kidney would be, a rock from the attack stabbed into my skin. The blood starts dripping out on the ground. X is about to prepare an attack, but I use the last of my energy to use my implosion box attack. Knowing the power my attack can deal I caution X not to move. His usual smirk comes across his face.

"You think a pathetic move like that could get the best of me". He says.

It takes me a few seconds to realize what X's hand sign is for, Ikeya's Kimoshiran gateway attack. In an instant X is gone, I wait for him to appear somewhere but the portal in front of me doesn't disappear. I stay on guard even so.

"Students stay away". Ikeya says. "X didn't do it right he is now trapped with the demons I warned you about. The portal will only disappear when he dies or finds his way out".

Jet asks Ikeya if he will go down to get him, he merely shakes his head and walks out of the room. The students flock out of the training room. I find Sorona, Jet and Sange telling them to meet me in my room later.

When the three get there I tell them I want to go after X. They immediately object to what I've suggested.

"Why should we Shinruga, he's only tried to hurt or kill you since we started here". Jet says.

"I know but still we can't just leave him down there to die. He can still be saved from darkness and evil". I counter.

All three of them shake their heads, most likely still refusing to go along with my plan. Sorona speaks up and says that she would like to go get X. Sange and Jet finally agree to go and get X as well. We all compromise on going late at night and going to get X.

Around nine o' clock we all meet in the training center. We look around to make sure that no one is around. I'm about to go into the portal when Sorona's body falls to the ground beside me. Jet is behind her, Sange is about to rip his head off. His hand is up and he's knocked her out.

"Jet, what the hell did you do that for"? He asks enraged.

Jet explains that he doesn't want to take a chance of Sorona getting hurt or worse.

"All right let's go". Saying Hastily.

The three of us jump into the portal. It takes a few seconds for my eyes to adjust to the light. Were in a cell and X is there, beaten and bruised.

"I tried to fend them off but there's just too many. I don't have any more strength their last attack was the last one I could fend off. I tried to use the gateway move again but it wouldn't work for some reason". X says.

"Here you go some food and water". I say.

Looking around there isn't much just pieces of people rotting. The bars holding X captive look to be thousands of years old. The walls look to be stained with blood, and horror.

Jet ask X when the guards are scheduled to come again. Something he probably picked up being held prisoner in Pokera.

"Twenty minutes from now, three guards will come. I don't know what they are after but they desperately want it". He tells us. "They look in my cell over and over and beat me. Odd thing is they won't tell me what they want".

Sange gives him some of his energy but he's still in no condition to fight. Probably still weakened from our fight and all the beatings.

"Why'd you come here for me Shinruga"?

"No reason just can't see a perfectly strong Psychian going to waste. You have no idea who you are or where you come from, so you think you're alone. That's what friends are for just give me a chance".

The four of us get ourselves into position for when the guards come.

When the guards come I can hear them wondering where X has gone to. When they open the door we all surprise attack them. Sange and Jet take one each while X and I fight the last one. All of us work in perfect unison as we're fighting, watching each other's backs. I knock out the guard I'm fighting, while X and Sange stab another from behind. I look closely at one, they look as though they use to be human at one time but no more. X lifts me and yells at us all to get moving. Running through the corridors I can hear the guards alerting their people. It all looks the same in this place, most of the cells are empty but some are filled with people. Moaning and screaming for our help but there is no way we could rescue them all. Something stops me at the last cell, a hand that has grabbed my ankle. He calls my name but at first I don't recognize him. My second look I remember who he is, he used to live in Recnamorcen.

"Don't trust Ikeya he had me use that attack of his knowing I would mess it up. I've heard that you have a shard in your blade, watch him those Psychian's are the ones he's after". He says. "I am the last person down here please kill me. There is no way to save me".

He's begging me and I just don't know if I could do it. X grabs my shoulder and tells me that we got to go. I tell X to go ahead and try to find a way out being that there is no other place to go. We have run out of room and need to find a way out quick or we'll be dead.

"Please just kill me now". He begs.

Taking a shuriken out of my bag I aim it at his head. I can see the look in his eyes, thankful for ending his life. This way he has to feel no more pain and torture. I throw my projectile it hits him right in the head. I can see the smile across his face as his eyes fade to darkness. Now he is free, free from their torture and evil.

"Come on Shinruga". Jet yells. "We found a door over there".

I run over to where the door is on the ceiling. X and Sange try turning the handle but it won't budge. Jet tries to use his energy to get it open but it still won't open. The cannibals are coming closer to us now. Every second we waste just brings us one step closer to doom.

"All four of us at the same time blast the door open". I say.

The four of us charge up a lot of energy and direct it to the door. The door blasts open I send X up first being he has so little energy left. Next Sange goes up, I'm about to send Jet up but he tells me to go first he will fend the beasts off. Going up the ladder I look down to see Jet turn into Phercon form. The beasts are about a hundred yards away from us. Jet opens his mouth and fires a blast of energy, hitting half of the cannibalistic beast. Jet turns back to normal and hurries up the ladder. When he gets out of the hole we try to close the door but the beast are pushing their way out. We keep kicking them down and finally they fall back into the hole. We close the door and it disappears.

What, where'd it go"? Jet asks.

"Not sure but we better get back to the school before we get caught". I say.

As we're running back to the school a kunai is thrown in front of us.

"Is it Ikeya"? ask X.

A man in a hood lands on the ground before us.

"This one escaped he will answer all your questions that you have". He says while throwing one of the beasts in front of us.

X picks him up pointing his blade at his face.

"If you don't tell me everything you know I'll kill you". He threatens.

The creature tells us a story about a young Psychian who invented a move to where he could travel from one to place to other using portals. When he goes into the wrong area and is captured he makes a deal to survive. When the guards bring him to their master he tells him that he will lure Psychian's down there to feed him and his people. This Psychian also pairs up with the AU to ensure his survival.

"Ikeya, everything you're telling us is about him". I say.

The beast nods his head and closes his eyes as X drives his sword into his head.

"Who are you"? Sange ask.

"My name is Karepth. I am from the Ghost Klan a society that watches over those with Shards in their swords. My master is intrigued by you Shinruga, we have found all but two of the people with shards".

Without realizing it, X and my blades are glowing again. Karepth notices this as well, his eyes light up.

"There's one more right there". He says. "X, that's your name isn't it".

X throws up his hand and fills it with energy and blast at Karepth. He easily dodges the blast and in a flash knees X in the gut. Karepth was so fast I couldn't even see him.

"Tell your friend Shinruga never to step in my way again or any of my people". He says.

I go over to tend X. Karepth puts his hand up and throws down something that explodes and blinds us all. When are sight returns we start riding our blades back to the school. We get there just before sunrise but are met at the wall by Ikeya. I stay on guard with the information I just learned.

"Leave this school you are no longer learning anything here". He says.

"No way, you just left him down there to die, we did your job. Rescuing X was supposed to be your job". I say.

"There is only one way for you to get back into my school...Fight me tomorrow eleven o' clock, all four of you".

I nod my head; Jet and Sange go back to their rooms. Still having X on my shoulders, I take him to the infirmary so he can be healed. The nurses lay him out on a table and tell me he will be healed tomorrow by the time of the fight. Satisfied with what I've heard I go back to my room to sleep, the intercom goes on and its Ikeya telling us that class is cancelled today. I lay my head down to go to sleep.

Waking up in the afternoon I notice that Jet is already up and gone. Asking around I find out that Ikeya has allowed us to go out of the school for one day. I'm also told that Jet, Sange and Sorona are on a hill overlooking the school.

When I arrive I am greeted by Sorona who gives me a hug. The others tell me a few strategies to beating Ikeya. In the end we all decide it will be up to luck and skill. Sange tells me that they have not told Sorona the information the beast told us. After a few minutes I explain it to her. She is appalled by what I tell her.

"Well it would seem that Ikeya is a traitor, there have been rumors but no one was for sure. Around Shiran he's been caught with some pretty shady people". She says.

Sange ask me about how X is doing. I assure him that X is fine. We all sit on the top of the hill watching the students come back into the school. We wait a few more minutes and go back into the school. Sange catches X walking in the crowd. He looks as though he's perfectly fine.

"Are you ok X"? Sorona asks.

"Yeah, I feel a lot better the nurses fixed me up great".

He tells us that he is completely healed for the fight tomorrow, and Ikeya better be ready. We all go back to our rooms and prepare for our fight tomorrow.

"Do you think we can win Shinruga"? Jet ask.

"I'm not sure but I hope so". I say.

Jet and I lay are heads down and rest our eyes.

CHAPTER 8

A MASTER'S ANGER

The next day there is no horn for us to wake up, the fight is today. Ikeya will be able to pound on us and make an example of the students who disobeyed his orders. I'm not sure if us four could go toe to toe with him or not. He's a master which means he knows skills that we've never heard of.

"Shinruga, you up"? Ask Jet.

I tell him I'm awake and that he needs to get dressed it's only an hour before the fight starts. We meet up with X, Sange and Sorona in the south hallway. X looks as though he's fully healed, it's good we're going to need him.

"It's time to fight you four". Ikeya says.

The four of us go into the training center and wait for all of the students to pile in. When all the students are in the training center Ikeya asks them to back up against the wall. Then he puts his hand up and tells the four of us once his hand goes down the fight will start.

"You guys ready"? I ask.

The three of them nod their heads. I also remind X that Ikeya will be centering his attention on the two of us. He nods again and waits for Ikeya to start the match.

"Time to feel some pain". Ikeya says coldly.

His hand falls and in not even one he's already to me. His fist pounds into my face and I go flying. Before Ikeya can land another blow on me X has caught up with him. They tussle for a few seconds but Ikeya throws X to the ground. Jet and Sange shoot energy blast from afar but Ikeya merely dodges and pursues after them. X and I run to help, I send an earth block after him. He dodges the attack and it almost hits Jet but it misses him as well. The four of us got Ikeya surrounded, we charge but he can keep up. X lands a hit on his face it knocks him to the ground, using his Kimoshiran Gateway attack he vanishes. We all turn in a different direction to find out where he has gone to.

"Where is he"? Sange ask.

We hear Ikeya from above just as we're all hit with a blast. I regain myself just fast enough to register Ikeya's foot to my face. He's about to strike me again but X has grabbed him from behind. X jumps backwards to slam Ikeya to the ground. Ikeya manages to pull out his blade and stop X. When Sange and Jet charge Ikeya it becomes a four way sword match. Ikeya is able to free our swords from our hands and knock us all back.

"Be careful you guys he has a needle sword that makes him very accurate". I remind the three.

Ikeya has charged up an energy blast and sends it over our heads. It explodes raining blast over us. He misses me, I charge but Ikeya merely grabs my shoulders and throws me to the ground again. He charges up energy in his hand, the energy burns when it hits. Before Ikeya can seriously hurt me Jet blasts him back.

"Shinruga, you okay"? Sange asks.

"Yeah, I'm all right". I respond.

"Ikeya put a lot into that blasts he used on you". Sange says.

The damage is apparent when I get up, my legs stammer into position. Sange puts his hand on my shoulder and gives me some energy. X and Jet are tag teaming Ikeya. X fires off an energy blast, while Jet distracts him. Jet moves Ikeya into position it hits him on his back. He falls to the ground and all four of us sweep in but Ikeya uses his Kimoshiran Gateway move again. This time we all put shields up to defend ourselves. Ikeya comes up behind X, I see him just in time to throw a shuriken. X finally realizes that Ikeya is behind him after I throw my shuriken behind him. He turns off his shield and backs up.

"Time for my new attack". X says.

X fills his hand with energy and when it forms the shape of an artistic X, he puts in one on his left hand on and one on his right hand. There is an immediate change in his energy level. He makes two more and puts them on his legs.

"I call them my X power patches, now I'm ten times stronger and faster". He says.

Ikeya nods and waits for X to attack. When he attacks Ikeya is barely able to block his attack, the rest of us join in the fray. With X's new amplified power the four of us start to wear Ikeya down. X and I land good solid hits on our master's face and gut. He falls to the ground we all throw a blast of energy at him, he spins circling with energy. X and Ikeya struggle for a few seconds but Ikeya is the victor. He elbows X to the face and then tackles him, while still keeping the three of us on guard by firing energy blasts.

My body feels weak but I shrug it off. When the blast stop I charge but Ikeya is already at my face.

"You think you can beat me"? Ikeya questions.

His fists connect with my stomach and then a foot to my face again. It sends me flying but Jet catches
me.

"Ikeya's really taking out on you man". Jet says.

"Yeah, no kidding. Here he comes again".

Ikeya is like a train; no matter what we throw at him he just bats it away. I put my hands to the ground and absorb the rock encasing my hands in earth. He's so fast but my eyes can keep up, Jet turns into his Phercon beast form to fight. X and Sange are now there to help, we start wearing Ikeya down. The four of us over power Ikeya, he powers up forcing us to back up.

"Now that he's more powerful, we have to be on even more guard". Thinking to myself.

"This ends now you four". Ikeya says. His voice angered by rage.

In a flash Ikeya is in the middle of the four of us. He fills his hands with energy and spins hitting all four of us. He throws a handful of needles at Jet and I. Pulling out my sword I'm able to stop them from hitting me in the head. Jet still being in Phercon form takes to fighting Ikeya on his own but is soon brought to the ground by a fury of blows. Once again Ikeya pursues me I can't keep from getting hit by most of his blows. Ikeya rains down more blasts of energy, the damage I've received is incredible. My body is frail and weak. X, Sange and Jet once again keep Ikeya off of me. Jet stops to tend to my wounds.

"You fine"? He asks.

"Yeah, I was hoping he would be too weak to fight him. I got two more moves that might even the playing field". I tell him. "What about that move you used yesterday where you shot energy out of your mouth".

"I could do it, just need to turn back into Phercon form". He says.

"For my second move I'm going to need Ikeya distracted, it's too powerful to miss him. Let go".

I use my first attack my Implosion box on Ikeya.

"Pathetic let's see what you can really do". Ikeya yells.

Clenching my hands together the box explodes. It sends Ikeya flying damaged but still filled with power. His hair is all over the place and his clothes are torn. Before he can unleash an onslaught on me X steps in his way but to no avail Ikeya knocks him to the ground. Once again I become his victim of rage, one hit and then another till I collapse to the ground. He pulls out his sword and is about ready to stab me when I see the line of energy comes across and hit Ikeya. Jet has turned back into Phercon form again. His energy is to low though so he has to turn back.

"You ready to do that move of yours? The three of us can keep Ikeya busy long enough to allow you to pull it off". Jet says.

"It's time for all of you to use all your energy and to use your best skills". I tell them.

"I will I've been saving some energy just in case". Sange says.

Ikeya charges Sange and Jet go forth to fight but it isn't any time before they are brought to the ground by Ikeya's wrath. X stayed behind with me to ensure my safety for at least a few seconds. Ikeya kicks X in the gut and elbows him in the back his patches disappear from his hands and legs. I fight with Ikeya for a few seconds but he trips me.

"My superior may have wanted you alive but killing you will be such a joy". Ikeya says.

He pulls out his sword and puts it up in the air, ready to stab me. I can see the end of his blade about to come down and pierce my heart.

Jet thankfully comes to my rescue with an energy field he rams Ikeya from behind sending him flying. Jet charges up an enormous energy blast in his hand and sends it in Ikeya's direction. The explosion's force causes me to close my eyes.

"I think now would be a good time to get that attack of yours going". Jet says.

I take his advice, taking out a bottle containing lightning. Charging up energy in one of my hands I ask Jet to open the bottle for me. When he does the lightning starts pouring out onto the ground around me and then to my hand. I put both my hands just above my waist and start spinning my hands.

"What is that thing"? Jet asks still waiting for Ikeya.

"It's called the Electric Psych Ball, my ultimate attack. As I harness the energy and purify it the ball gets a ring around it. The more rings the more powerful". I explain.

Jet asks me how long it's going to take the attack to reach full power. The normal is five minutes per ring.

My old master Sochajo taught me this move I was his star pupil. It's an extremely dangerous move to attempt; if your energy and lightning aren't completely synchronized it will blow up in your face. It was several tries before I got this move right. Now I have to use it as a last resort because there is one down fall to this attack. The user has to sacrifice twenty percent of his life energy.

As the second ring forms around my attack I can see Ikeya managing to pull himself from the rubble. We can hear him muttering some words from across the training center as he walks closer.

"Jet, Sange, X. You guys have to keep him busy one of you is going to have to hold him right until the blast is close". I say.

Ikeya's eyes go wide when he realizes what attack I'm about to fire at him. He powers up to his remaining level knowing how much damage my attack could inflict on him. Ikeya charges with rage in his eyes, X and Sange meet him about twenty feet away from me. He easily evades their attacks charging up a blast in one hand hitting X and kicks Sange in the head. Jet uses the remaining power he has to turn back into Phercon form. Ikeya uses an attack that turns his whole body into needles. Even Jet's Phercon form is no match for Ikeya. Ikeya's next attack sends Jet up into the air, to finish his attack he shoots all the needles at Jet. Jet somehow blocks most of them with an energy shield but some of them hit his arms. He cries out in pain as he falls to the ground, Ikeya lands in front of him and puts his hand out.

"You pest". Ikeya says.

Ikeya lets the energy flow out of his hands. Once again I can hear Jet cry out in agony. I yell for Ikeya to come to me. Somehow he throws a needle right through my attack hitting me in the shoulder. I almost lose control of my attack but I stick it out. The third ring is now complete and I'm ready to fire the attack at Ikeya but knowing him he will just dodge it. Noticing Jet behind Ikeya I use my feet to send some energy his way. I'm struggling but I fire my Electric Psych ball, as I predicted Ikeya moves to his right.

"All that preparing and you missed". Ikeya chuckles.

The blast goes towards Jet and I yell out to him. Jet with the energy I gave him creates a shield which bounces the attack back at its original target.

I fall to the ground and wait for Ikeya to come kill me.

"Fool now you die...What the"?

Ikeya notices the energy behind him, he tries to put up a shield but it's destroyed the second the attack hits. The explosion is huge, we wait for the dust to clear and when it does our blades are at Ikeya's face before he can move. His body is frail and limp the damage that has been dealt looks as though it's crippled him. He's able to get on one knee.

"Congrats, you four you can stay. Can we get some nurses in here"? Ikeya yells.

Four nurses come out of the infirmary I can hear the students going wild as Ikeya's words are spoken. Sorona comes over to the four of us and congratulates us. I'm so weakened from the fight before I can thank her I slip into the darkness.

CHAPTER 9

SHINRUGA'S SECRET

I awake in the middle of the day with Sorona and Jet hovering over my bed. They ask me how I'm feeling but the signs are obvious. My wounds show my bruised and beaten body.

"Holy cow, what was that attack"? Jet asks.

Still delirious from my fight I have trouble remembering what attack he's talking about.

"The one with the electricity and your energy"? He says.

I explain my destructive attack to Jet and Sorona. Jet's mouth goes wide with envy.

The next few days there is no class due to the injuries Ikeya received from the fight. It takes me two days before I can finally get out of the bed and walk on my own, with the assistance of a crutch though. On my third day of being in the infirmary Yamasaki pays me a visit. He tells me that he wants to fight X and I one on one. At first I decline but what he promises to give me is too valuable to pass up. Yamasaki sets the day for three days from now. After a couple of more days I can finally walk without a crutch and I'm feeling pretty good. Classes are still cancelled on account that Ikeya is still bed ridden from our fight. For the next couple of days all I can hear from the other students is the news of my upcoming fight. It's not too long before Sorona and Jet are bugging me about it. The next day I'm out in the north courtyard sword handling. The place is a sight to behold the Procker trees in the wind, there fruit scattered on the ground. Procker trees rose from the ground after humans practically died off. The fruit is red like an apple but as big as a pineapple the taste is bitter though. Most people and Psychian's use it in soups. There is a fountain of a man with messed up blonde hair and what looked to be green eyes, the whole thing is starting to wear away. I sense someone come up behind me. I spin my sword the blade is nearly at her throat. Sorona is standing in front of me with a smile on her face.

"Glad to see your senses are still as keen as ever". She says.

"No shield, no sword of your own pulled out pretty risky wouldn't you say".

"Not really".

She asks me if I'm ready for the fight tomorrow. The fight I almost completely forgot. I go back to training while Sorona keeps talking to me. She says my name quietly as if someone was watching.

"Do you have a sister"? She asks.

The question about floors me to the ground. I ask her how she knows this information. She tells me that someone close to her family told her and Sange. My eyes are glued to the ground I only awake from this world when Sorona gives me a little push. She has a little smirk on her face and keeps asking if I'm all right.

"It was ten years ago she was the star pupil of my master and the hopeful to end the AU but she got careless. She heard a rumor that Kita was most likely to be their next leader. She stormed out of the house in the middle of the night. It was two days after that they found her body or what was left of it".

"Why, have I never heard of this before"? She asks.

"The family kept it hidden to the rest of the world, as far as they know she's just lost or captured but not dead. We let the world make up their own stories".

"Why, not tell them though instead of hiding it"? She asks.

"Not sure guess the family is a little embarrassed or they can't let go of her still". I say.

Sorona shakes her head a little and leaves.

I sit on the edge of the fountain with my head now full of memories I've forgotten for a long time. My sister born twelve years before I. A prodigal Psychian who at my current age contained twenty times the strength that I have. It was a dark stormy night I was only five but I can remember it clear as day. She stormed out of her room and throughout the living room and towards the door. Our father's hand grabs her arm and stops her. My father catches her stern look across her face right before she gives him a blast to the stomach. He chases her outside and knocks her to the ground. She has tears in her eyes I can't hear what they are saying but in the next couple of days I have an idea. Two days after my sister left the town of Shiran it was attacked and reduced to rubble. Five days after we moved out of Shiran in are new town of Recnamorcen. I was outside behind our house about to get a drink from a stream when I saw her lifeless corpse. The left arm and leg were cut off. Two days after that her funeral was held only Furrock and Sounni and my family attended. Since her death I've always tried to take life a little less seriously. My growing strength I guess concerns people that I will become her.

I depart from the courtyard and go back into the school. I'm walking by Ikeya's room when I can hear a dark voice come from inside. The door is open so I take a peek inside, a book shelf in the far corner is to the left and a pathway leads downstairs. The deep voice is so evil my gut starts to churn in pain. I see a shadow on the stair walls and I sense Ikeya's presence coming up the stairs. I duck behind the wall and wait for Ikeya to close the door. The rattling of the door closing makes enough noise so that I can escape without alerting Ikeya. I get back to my room and close the door as quickly as possible. Not too long afterwards someone comes knocking at my door. I'm on guard as I turn the handle but when it opens I'm surprised to see Yamasaki in front of me.

"I came here to remind you of our fight tomorrow, you do remember right"? He says.

"I remember but why do you want to fight X and me so badly"? I ask.

"Like I said my master is very interested in the two of you, he wants to know how much power you posses so far".

He's about to ask me another question when he looks to his right and his eyes go wide.

"What is it"? I ask.

I go out to the hallway to see and there he is Kita. The students have formed lines on each side of him.

"Shinruga, how nice to see you again". He says sarcastically.

My hands fill with energy because I'm about to attack but Ikeya calls my name. I stop the energy from coming out of my body. Ikeya puts his arm on Kita's shoulder and signals for him to come to his chambers.

"I don't get it why is Kita here and why is Ikeya acting like they are best friends, maybe Kita is threatening Ikeya". He says.

"I doubt it, Ikeya is evil and I have the proof".

He doesn't believe me at first but after I tell the story that the creature from below told us.

"I have to go warn my master of this or else more students could be lured into his trap. This will be his last year he will teach. Once my master comes here he will shut this school down".

"How, only the triple Psychian can enforce rules and laws". I say.

After the fall of humans, their government seemed to cease to exist. People and Psychian's alike started to try and form their own laws. The triple Psychian thought otherwise being that he was pure of heart suggested that only he make rules. When a problem occurred he'd be the solution but he died before the rules were set into place. It wasn't too long afterwards that the new laws were placed into order. There are different rules for people and Psychian's. A lot of the old laws that humans had before we existed still exist. When the new triple Psychian comes around he or she has a lot of work to do.

"Listen Shinruga my master Hiraski has been helping watch over you and your family". He says. "My master is one of the reasons that you're still alive, he saved your father's life at least three times".

I search through all the memories in my head, no mention of the name Hiraski comes to mind. Not one after a few seconds of thinking I shrug it off.

Kita finally leaves the room with a satisfied look on his face. Kita once again stops when he's beside me.

"Oh, and Shinruga say hi to Furrock for me". He says.

What Kita says chills me straight to the bone. Does this mean he knows where Furrock and Sounni live? Kita keeps walking with all the students staring angrily at him. The famed new Psychian killer walking right beside us.

Yamasaki walks up beside me again.

"I have warned my master he should be here tomorrow before our fight. You know of Ikeya's secret room the demon creatures and the deep evil power". He asks.

"Yes I do I've been on the other side of that door". I say.

Yamasaki leaves for other business as I go back into my room. Jet soon arrives in our room to go to sleep and as do I.

My night is full of new nightmares, I'm the Triple Psychian and Kita is in front of me. His black formal suit with four buttons down the middle and his black slacks. He's standing in front of me not a scratch on him, my body bruised and beaten. He stands over me and just before his blade goes into my head, I'm woken up.

Jet is huddled over me telling me to wake up.

"It's not too long before yours and Yamasaki's fight". Jet says.

Jet and I are about to go to the North courtyard when Yamasaki's hand stops us.

"My master is here, come look". Yamasaki says.

We go into the main corridor and see a man standing in front of Ikeya. Hiraski has long brown hair, samurai armor and almost an exact replica to Yamasaki's dragon blade.

"Is that him"? I ask.

"No, that's not him".

"To all of you students my name is Hiraski and after the next two days Ikeya's school will be no more". He says.

Hiraski walks over to the three of us.

"Master Aitaku has gone rogue and evil I've taken over now". He says.

"And who has given you the right to say my school has to be taken down"? Ikeya asks.

"By these written laws passed down to my superiors over time. Those who obey the homicidal and evil die". Hiraski says.

"Sounds like to me your trying to take the Triple Psychian's place. I am one of the royals, you cannot question my loyalty".

"I am direct descendant of the Triple Psychian". Claims Hiraski.

"How would he know that information, the Triple Psychian had no family I thought"? I say.

"Hiraski and Aitaku is the information hub of the world". Yamasaki says.

"Shut down peacefully or face the consequences Ikeya". Hiraski warns.

Without saying a word Ikeya charges at Hiraski, he ducks our master's attack and puts an energy ball to his stomach. The energy ball has something glowing in the middle. The attack sends Ikeya flying to the wall when he hits the energy ball opens up. Life energy rains upon Ikeya. Damaged from the attack Ikeya falls to ground he stammers to get up.

"Time to end your career Ikeya"! Hiraski yells.

A shield goes above all of the student's heads, as Hiraski uses his energy to destroy the roof of the training center.

Yamasaki pulls out a hand tazer to put on Ikeya but right when he's about to Ikeya reaches in his shirt and throws a smoke pellet to the ground. Hiraski and Yamasaki frantically look to find Ikeya but cannot see him. The roof of the training center comes barreling down. All the students are in a panic as to what's happened. Hiraski and Yamasaki come walking over to me followed by Sorona and Sange.

"Shinruga, heard a lot about you my name is Hiraski the leader of the school in Saya. I'd be honored if you attend my school your friends Sorona and Sange as well. From what I understand Jet is already a Shogun".

I look over to see Yamasaki with his usual grin.

"In the next few days my team will come destroy this place and bury the doors to which those creatures can get out. Yamasaki is one of my prized students and is cooperating to help that the next Triple Psychian doesn't turn evil. Jet if you want to go see a great teacher and help the cause go visit Master Itchitori in this city on the map".

Saya is a two month trip, past the major cities and is out in the middle of nowhere. We will surely run into trouble, which doesn't seem to bother me.

Hiraski hands me a piece of paper which is marked where Saya is located. The two of them walk out of the corridor and into the student's rooms.

X soon joins around us and we tell him of the information we've learned. Jet and I soon go back to our room and start packing up our stuff. We meet X, Sange and Sorona outside of the school. The five of us turn to take one last look at our old school before we depart to Furrock's house.

CHAPTER 10

YAMASAKI'S MIGHT

When the five of us get to Furrock's house, I knock on the door. He answers with a surprised look on his face.

"What are you kids doing here"? He asks.

He invites us in to his house and offers us something to eat and drink.I fill him in to what has happened at the school. The fact doesn't startle him too much, I suspect that he's had people check up on Ikeya. I'm only in the house for a few minutes till I can't contain myself anymore.

"Where's Sounni at"? I ask.

Furrock tells me that she's gone to the market and won't be back for a while.

There's a knock at the door, all of us are on guard. When Furrock opens the door Hiraski is standing there with his hands behind his back.

"May I see Shinruga and the other four"? He inquires.

Furrock gives him a puzzled look but before he can ask who he is Hiraski introduces himself.

"Excuse me Shinruga, Jet, Sorona, X, and Sange you left before I could tell you this. School is still open for another two days till my troop gets here. Just bring enough stuff for two more days. My second mastery is the Kimoshiran form. You can come anytime just be there by tonight". He informs.

We nod our heads in approval and start packing the little stuff we need. I'm walking out and yell to Hiraski but the sight of Sounni distracts me.

"Yes Shinruga can I help you"? Hiraski ask.

I wave him away hoping that he won't get mad. He politely nods and goes about his business.

Sounni comes running over to me and leaps into my arms.

"I missed you so much". She says.

It's the only thing she says to me till we get into town. We browse the market looking at all the shelves but nothing is to appealing. Before we head home we stop at the tree that we spent the night sleeping together. Seeing that it is nearly dark I remind Sounni that I have to go she grabs my arm tighter as we're walking. When we get back to Furrock's house Sounni kisses me and tells me not to die in the next couple of days. I'm about halfway there when Jet yells my name. When I turn to look Sorona is draped over his arms, she looks lifeless.

"What happened"? I ask running over to them.

"I'm not sure. I was coming here and I saw her lying on the ground". Jet replies.

We both agree to get her to Master Hiraski as soon as possible. When we get to our former school we can see about ten guys standing outside of the school. We approach but one of the guys puts his hand out, more than likely a guard of Hiraski's.

"Shinruga Deshreneto, you may proceed. Who are these and what happened to the girl"? He asks.

The guard is enormous, his whole body and face is full of scars. He bears Hiraski's mark though so I know we can trust him.

"I am Jet and this is Sorona we both attended this school, now if you don't mind we need to get through to take her to Hiraski". Jet says angrily.

The guards let us through we run as fast as we can to Hiraski. He asks us both what happened to Sorona. Jet puts his head down and almost starts to cry but before he can Hiraski grabs his arm.

"I will fix her don't worry". He says.

Hiraski puts his hands just above Sorona's and adds energy to his hands. He goes up and down her body several times and just before we think he's done his energy pulls out three needles from her side. I pick up one of the needles and realize who's they are.

"I recognize them anywhere, its Ikeya's". I say.

Hiraski gets up and waves his hand, the shadow on the wall begins to take form. Yamasaki is standing in front of us all.

Yamasaki leans over and Hiraski tells him something, in a flash he's gone. Hiraski tells us that the whole town will now be on guard watching for Ikeya. Sange comes bursting through the door he cradles Sorona in his arms begging that she'll be all right. Hiraski assures Sange that he has done everything he needs to, to save her life.

"Now all she needs is some rest and her wounds will be healed by morning". Hiraski says.

Jet asks Sange if it would be all right if he could sleep with her tonight. Sange nods and they take her to her bedroom. Hiraski reminds them that a nurse will be in the next room so as nothing will go wrong.

"Why, if he stabbed the needles in her why beat her up like that". I ask.

"To make it look as though it was just a robbery or a thug attack. Ikeya's smart if those needles had been in there much longer she would've died. It's late you should be getting to bed now. After all you have a fight tomorrow". He says.

Did Yamasaki tell Hiraski of our fight? Is our fight still going to happen, why does he want to fight so badly? These questions plague me all night, who is Hiraski, why is he so interested in me? I stay up for several hours but the questions keep coming and to no avail does an answer arise. When I finally do get to sleep it's filled with the same nightmare of Kita and me fighting.

Shoving from my left side awakes me from my slumber. My eyes open to see Jet's familiar face. He reminds me that Yamasaki and X's fight is in about an hour. It takes me some time to get ready by the time I finally get to the training center most of the students are already there standing in a circle. X and Yamasaki are standing in the middle of them. Hiraski grabs my shoulder and explains the rules.

"There will be nothing above a mid level attack in this fight". He says. "I want to see what the two of you are capable of without using your highest level attacks".

Hiraski walks into the middle of Yamasaki and X. He explains the rules one more time to the two of them, X and Yamasaki both nod their heads in acknowledgement.

Looking around the room I can that there is almost nothing left of the training center. Most of the roof is gone and a lot of the support beams are scarred. By looking though I can see that there are quite a few advantages to the new landscape.

Hiraski steps back a few feet and calls for them to fight. X as usual uses all his speed to get right up to Yamasaki. Before X can manage to throw more than a few punches Yamasaki's knee connects to his gut. He stammers backwards and powers up some energy. This time it's Yamasaki who charges X punches the ground sending an earth wave at his opponent.

"He's already lost". Hiraski says.

"How"? Jet asks.

"X always relied on his anger to power him through his fights now that it's gone he's off of his game. He needs to find something else to fill the void of where his anger was. When two people are fighting and one of them is off their game it's very easy to tell who is going to win". Hiraski explains.

I turn my head back to the fight, X is getting pounded. All of his attacks are just sloppy to say the least. Hiraski nudges my arm to remind me that I'm up next to fight.

Turning my attention back to the fight I can see that X is away from Yamasaki. He is rapidly firing off energy blast, the sure sign of a Psychian's desperation. Yamasaki simply avoids the blasts, jumps into the air and rains fire upon X. X focuses his energy into a shield, when the fire dissipates X attacks. He throws an onslaught of punches and energy blasts. Yamasaki merely blocks and deflects his attacks. Yamasaki gets close to X and before X can use another attack Yamasaki puts his hand on the ground. A piece of earth comes up from the ground; it's in the shape of a dragon.

"I wouldn't say that's exactly mid level"? I say.

"For Yamasaki it is. It's one of my attacks I found a new way to manipulate the earth making it easier to conjure up animals". Hiraski explains.

X forges a few of his power patches but before he can even plant them on his hands, Yamasaki's dragon knocks him to the ground. X summons all the energy in his body to blast the dragons face. The dragon turns to dust.

"Where are you"? X yells in rage.

X turns his head every way to see where Yamasaki is located. He finally senses Yamasaki's presence, it's too late. The tip of Yamasaki's blade is at X's nose.

"This fight is over". Hiraski yells.

X steps back I can see that his anger is growing. The look in his eyes the same look that he gave me when we fought. His hands charge up with energy. Hiraski steps in the middle of the two of them. He tells X that if he attacks he will chop his arm off. X finally backs down and starts walking back to the school. Hiraski grabs his shoulder and says something below a whisper. X continues to walk into the school.

Hiraski turns his attention back to the students. He points to me and directs me to fight.

"Hopefully you can present me with a better challenge". Yamasaki says.

"Don't worry that won't be a problem". I say.

Hiraski once again steps in between and reminds us of the rules. He tells us both to get ready to fight.I charge my hands with energy and wait for Yamasaki to attack.

A single leaf from a Maplech tree falls signaling for our fight to begin. Yamasaki shoots at me like a bullet I block his oncoming kick to my side. Grabbing his leg I throw him onto the ground. Shooting several blasts Yamasaki dodges them, and fires back with a dagger of ice. I draw my sword and slice it in half. The two pieces turn to water Yamasaki comes to fight once again. My feet won't budge, when I look down. There is a sheet of ice sticking me to the ground. By the time my eyes catch Yamasaki's figure he's only a few feet away. With my sword still in hand I hold it up to defend myself. His attack is vicious, when our swords connect sparks and lightning starts shooting out. The crowd is going nuts with excitement. It doesn't take too long before the lightning is hitting the ice to which has encased my feet. When Yamasaki finally backs off, I hit the ice off of my feet. We lock swords again for a few seconds I'm winning but with a quick maneuver, our swords go flying. Yamasaki leaps forward tackling me to the ground. He tries to punch me in the face but I put my hands to the ground putting a shield of earth over me. Lunging onto Yamasaki I pin the earth to his body, trapping him there. I fill my hands with energy punching Yamasaki's face as many times as I can. He powers up and his power is so incredible it breaks the earth and I off of Yamasaki.

"Simple moves like that won't work". Yamasaki says panting.

"I hope not". I say.

Yamasaki stares me down for a few seconds but this time I charge. I use my arm to fake an attack but sweep his leg with mine. He falls to the ground, before I can land another hit he's already up. With a concentrated energy blast it barely misses my head. He's too quick for my eyes to follow Yamasaki lands two good hooks to my cheeks. The punches send me to the ground I roll backwards and am quickly on guard. Yamasaki's coming at me once again; he fills both hands with energy and fires a fury of blast. Thinking quickly, I duck behind a piece of the debris left over from the training centers roof. I can feel that the piece of debris is crumbling with every blast. Yamasaki appears in front of me firing some more blasts, the blasts are still coming from behind as well. I jump to the right and take refuge behind another piece of stone. I notice that my sword is stabbed into the ground right beside me. I take a peek my assumption was right a blast sitter.

Blasts sitters are a common trick by Psychian's, by focusing your energy and leave it one spot. As much energy as the Psychian puts in it the blast sitter will fire.

I stand charging at the blast sitter deflecting the blast coming out of it. Yamasaki tries to intervene but I send an earth wave at him. I slice the sitter in half the remaining power explodes in my face. I take cover within the smoke. Giving Yamasaki no time to think I fire several blasts at him. They go whizzing by his head. After his confusion has kicked in I strike with my sword. He of course is on guard and blocks the strike with ease.

"Petty attacks like that will have no effect". Yamasaki says with a smirk.

Yamasaki and I are still gridlocked when my energy blasts come back. Yamasaki somehow senses them and jumps backwards. I can't move out of the way in time and hold my hands out; I slide backwards for a few seconds and use my hands to send them flying upwards. I shake my hands of the heat but before I can take a second to relax Yamasaki is already closing in. He pulls out his sword once more and holds it over his head. Yamasaki's handles his sword so easy and fast that I cannot keep up. The last swing of his sword catches my chest cutting my shirt and leaving a small slice on my chest. The crowd falls silent as I sink to the ground on my right knee.

"Easy Yamasaki this is only a sparring match". Yells Hiraski.

"Sorry sir won't happen again". Yamasaki says.

After taking a few seconds to apply some energy over my wound, I finally rise to my feet. Yamasaki is staring me down; I decide it's ready to show my full power.

"It's time Yamasaki you saw what I'm really capable of". I say.

His usual smirk disappears as I put my hands into fist. Then the dark purple energy starts flowing out of my body. The grass below my feet starts to rise from the intensity of my power. Yamasaki is now on guard and waiting for me to attack. When I'm done everything and everybody can feel my new power.

"Do you think that stand a chance now Yamasaki"? I ask.

"We will see". He says.

I put my hands into fighting position and charge. The first few hits connect with Yamasaki's face, leaving him dazed. He quickly recovers and blocks the next few.

"Did you really think the power that I was using, was the extent of what I'm capable of"? Yamasaki asks.

Yamasaki and I are now gridlocked with our hands. He also powers up, I can feel the intensity. The power that he is emitting is pushing on my chest. I flip backwards adding energy to my boots, the shields from the boots hit him square in the chin. Jumping forward I tackle him to the ground but Yamasaki quickly frees himself from my hold. The next thing I can feel is his foot landing on the side of my face. I regain my footing and put my hands out. Yamasaki does the same and we both fire off a blast of energy. When the two connect sparks go flying, for a few moments it appears as though the two are equal. Once again we both power up and the blast continues to grow in strength.

"Give up Yamasaki it's over". I yell.

Even though I know Yamasaki and my blasts are the same I try to make him doubt himself. We both try to put more energy into our blast but instead of it continuing to grow, the blast explodes. My vision is unclear from all the smoke around. Twisting my head from side to side my eyes still can't locate Yamasaki. To become clearer of my surroundings I close my eyes. It takes a few seconds but I finally pick up his location. Firing a blast from my hand it scares Yamasaki out of hiding. Yamasaki comes out from the smoke and slashes what he thinks is me. After he realizes it's only a stone figure, he looks every which way but it's too late. My right foot lands to his left temple. Yamasaki falls to the ground wrenching the left side of his face. By manipulating the wind I blow all the smoke away.

"I told you to give up". I brag.

Yamasaki powers up once again, his energy surging through his body. He bolts towards me I use my energy to create handholds in the air. When I get to the final hold, I jump to a railing of what use to be the roof of the training center. My climb is stopped short by Yamasaki, who somehow found a faster way up. With the look of rage in his eyes he fires off one blast after another. At first my thought is that he's trying to hit me but his plan becomes apparent. The blast hit above me hitting the cracked ceiling. Soon the ceiling and ladder start trembling, next they break apart. Now free falling through the air I push off of the ladder. The second my feet touch the ground I change into my Kimoshiran form, I form my hands into the necessary position for Kimoshiran gateway. My body sinks into the ground a second before the debris hits the ground.

"Yamasaki this is a sparring match". Hiraski yells.

"He's not finished". Yamasaki responds.

I can see Yamasaki looking around, now is the time to strike. I run out with my sword drawn, Yamasaki unsheathes his sword to block. Our swords connect with enough force to imprint the ground at our feet.

"You can't keep this up forever Shinruga". Yamasaki says.

"Neither can you, I can feel your power going down". I reply.

Yamasaki powers up his energy enough to fend our swords off of each other. We stand staring each other down, his dragon blade and my Monkey blade. I put out my sword and call out my attack.

"A dozen monkeys". I yell.

A dozen monkeys appear from the ground, they start circling around me. Their faces are cute and look as though they couldn't harm a fly. Once I point my sword to Yamasaki the monkeys faces change from cute and playful to horrific and evil. They charge at him climbing and jumping on anything and everything. Yamasaki's eyes are having a hard time focusing on all of them. He fires a few blasts from his hands and manages to hit a few but most of them are already by him. He puts his hand to the ground and summons another dragon made of earth. The dragon and monkeys fight for a little bit and I wait for them to get closer to Yamasaki. When they do I light them on fire, by making my hand into a fist the monkeys explode. I wait for the smoke to clear to locate my opponent. I stare into the smoke waiting for him but still nothing. My eyes catch a shadow I run towards it but instead of it being Yamasaki it's another earth dragon. When the dragon puts its head down I jump onto it. I can see Yamasaki with his hands full of energy. Pushing off of the dragons back I pull out my sword targeting Yamasaki.

"Now you're finished Shinruga". He says.

I'm about to put my sword into Yamasaki's chest, when he makes his blast bigger.

"Take this". Yamasaki says.

He fires his blast, before it can hit me I put out my left hand. Shooting energy to the ground I use it to swerve to the right. When I touch ground I put my sword to the back of his neck.

"You think that I'm done. I can just go forward". Yamasaki says.

"Try that with him on your chest". I say.

Looking on his chest Yamasaki can see the last monkey staring him down.

"What but how"? He says.

"This fight is over". Hiraski says.

Hiraski walks over to me from the sidelines. He congratulates me on winning the fight. He pulls a sword from his back and hands it to me. I accept the blade its hilt is made of a single wing and the handle looks as though it's dragon skin. The dragons head is at the bottom of the blades handle.

The students come over and shake my hand and pat my back congratulating me.

"All right Shinruga". Jet says.

I see Yamasaki walking away into the school. Catching up to him I grab his shoulder, he turns around asking what I want. He tells me that he was hoping that I would win, that the dragon blade will be of vital use to me.

"My sister was the same way, never could lose a fight". I say.

"Your sister, what happened to her"? He asks.

I tell him the story and he only says one thing, that he will look into it and he walks away.

Somehow my body lingers back to my room and into my bed. It doesn't take me much time to get to sleep, seeing as I just got out of a fight. I wait for the next day to come so that I can see Sounni again.

Chapter 11

Graduation

My usual nightmare awakes me from my slumber. Its graduation day all the students pack up their stuff and single file into the training center. When we walk into the training center there is a stage and Hiraski standing in the middle.

"You know how this works Shinruga". Hiraski says.

"Yeah". I say.

He nods and we go about our business. All the students sit in the chairs perfectly aligned. When all the students are sat down Hiraski walks off the stage and in front of the students.

"You students have been betrayed by your former teacher. In his office I have found papers on each of you students, your skills, and your attacks. Remember this, the ones who are against me want you dead. If your job is to kill your Psychian's, your kind. Unless you know they're evil, you're probably doing the wrong thing". Hiraski says.

Hiraski sets the papers down on the table in front of the students. He tells the students that we can come up and see our profiles. Hiraski pulls a clipboard from the table, gets back on the stage and starts calling the students name one by one. When the students get up on the stage they bow in front of Hiraski and then shake his hand. Almost all of the students who come off the stage check their profiles. It's now my turn to go up on the stage, when I get up there I bow as I'm supposed to and then I shake Hiraski's hand. When I do our hands light up with energy and then it's gone. This is the sign of a teacher graduating a student, only the teacher's know this secret code. When I get off of the stage I meet my friends who are also checking their profiles. In my profile I can see my name where I was born, my level of power, and everything there is to know about me. Jet and Sorona confirm that their profiles are the exact same. X has a weird look on his face, he looks around and when he thinks no one is looking he swipes his folder.

"Hey, Jet I'll meet you back at our room". I say.

Walking through the hallway I'm a little startled when X comes out of a shadow from a corner.

"You saw me take my folder didn't you"? X asks.

I nod my head in acknowledgement; he throws the folder at me. I take a quick gander, real name unknown, where he was born unknown; it all looks as mine does.

"Flip the paper over and look at the back and read it aloud". He says.

When I flip the paper and read the back I'm a little surprised.

"This student seems to show anger that if persuaded might be able to turn to our side. His power has risen exponentially since the school year has started. Upon more study his blade contains a Shard from the Triple Psychian".

X asks me if he thinks it's possible that he could be turned to the other side. I reassure X that from what I've seen he's not capable of turning to the other side. He tells me that he will see me around Shiran, he still has not decided what Psychian Warrior school he is going to.

When I finally get back to my room and pack up the few stuff I brought with me. Jet finally appears in the room and also packs his little bit of stuff. When were done packing we meet up with Sorona and Sange. We're just outside of the school when Yamasaki runs up to me.

"I almost forgot to give you this paper it's a map to get to Hiraski's town". He says.

He runs over to catch up with Hiraski and then they're off like the wind. We finally get to Furrock's house and I knock on the door. Sounni comes to the door, when she opens it she runs out and hugs Sorona. The two jump up and down in complete joy. She then runs over to me and jumps into my arms.

"Hey, the three of us are going to go over to Sorona's parents". Jet says.

Jet and I shake hands and bid each other a temporary farewell. When we walk into Furrock's house I'm greeted by a hug from Furrock.

"Sounni and I have an idea since you guys graduated from your Kimoshiran training we'll throw a graduation party". Furrock says.

Thinking that it's a great idea I give him my opinion. Sounni tells me though that the three of us are going to go out and go shopping together for the party. We eat some lunch and then start walking down the road to go shopping. Jet and Sorona meet us along the way, we clue them into what we are doing. When we get to town out of the corner of my eye I catch X standing in a line. We invite him to the party and ask if he will help us set up. He agrees to help us out with the party. While we're in town Jet pulls me aside into one of the markets and asks everyone for a little privacy.

"What is it"? I ask.

"Are you going to free Pokera now"?

"I wish we could right now but we're not strong enough. We wouldn't make it through the front door". I say.

His face goes from anticipation to sadness. I warn him not to worry about that right now. We catch up with the rest of our friends and continue shopping. In all of the rushing I yell out, forgetting that no one has invited my parents. Furrock tells me not to worry that he did it the day that him and Sounni came up with the idea. It's about four o'clock when we're done with the shopping and get back to Furrock's house. Taking our time and not rushing the decorating we get done in about an hour. X departs from the house about nine o'clock. Sorona and Sange leave an hour later. Furrock lets the three of us know that another hour and it's time to go to bed. There's a knock at the door it's from the letter givers.

The letter givers were made around the first twenty years of earth's revival. They were made to ensure that there was a way for people to keep in contact with each other. Most letters only take a day to receive but depending where you are and where it needs to go could take more.

"Shinruga, it's a letter for you". Furrock says.

The letter is from my mother and father.

"Son congratulations on finishing your Kimoshiran schooling. Beware of those who you can't trust. Your mother and I received a letter from master Hiraski. He's an old friend, when you're his student mind everything he says and don't embarrass me...Ha just kidding. I know you'll do fine my son. Love you from the both of us and we'll see you tomorrow". It reads.

I grip the letter hard in my hand. I have not seen my mother and father since I started school, my body can't help but to be excited to see them again. It's nearing the time to go to bed so I turn in early. Walking over to Sounni I bend over and give her a kiss. Noticing light out of the corner of my eye I can see energy coming from Furrock's hand. My first instinct being a fighter is to duck for cover. When I do Furrock burst out laughing and slapping his knee.

"Ha, ha, you should have seen you jump". Furrock says hysterically.

Sounni yells at her father reminding him that he shouldn't play practical jokes on me. Furrock assures her that he was just playing. I know that Furrock would never hurt me just for kissing her but it's still kind of annoying.

"You three time to go to sleep for the night". Furrock says.

Jet and I go back to our rooms, when my head hit's the pillow sleep immediately sets in. Due to nightmares my sleep is short lived. It's about three o'clock in the morning and I walk out of my room and outside. I sit on Furrock's porch which overlooks half of Shiran. Something about Furrock tells me this is no coincidence. While sitting there in his deck chair my eyes catch a shadow. I try to find it again but no luck only a voice.

"Shinruga, you fool, you think that I would leave so soon. First I have to kill you or else I will pay". The voice says.

My ears finally recognize the voice, it's Ikeya.

"Might want to leave Shiran, you're wanted by every Psychian in this city and all the rest of them". I say.

He's still not in sight even though I've looked everywhere. Finally my eyes see him, so I thought. It's not Ikeya it's a dart heading straight for me. My feet are glued to the ground though. This is the end of Shinruga Deshreneto, my life done at sixteen. The dart is just a few feet from my face now. Out of nowhere an energy wolf grabs the dart out midair. My feet release from the ground and just as they do Furrock bolts out the front door. He fires an enormous blast of energy at a nearby tree. That's when I can finally see Ikeya. From what I could see he's a little bruised and scuffed up. A branch from the tree Furrock shot breaks and crashes to the ground. Furrock makes another energy wolf and tells his two wolves to track Ikeya down. Furrock stands there perfectly still with his eyes closed. After a few seconds he opens his eyes.

"What happened"? I ask.

"Ikeya, killed the two wolfs but he's wounded". Furrock says.

Jet and Sounni finally come out of their rooms. Wondering what has just conspired. We fill them in on what just happened.

After a few seconds we all go into the kitchen and talk.

"Shinruga, until you're done with your Shogun teaching you should always have someone with you. That is when your power and fighting wisdom will be at their peak". Furrock says.

The four of us go to our rooms and return back to sleeping, a couple of hours later Sounni opens my door and comes into my room. I'm about to ask her what she's doing but she puts her hand over my mouth to silence me. She grabs my head and begins kissing me as if she will never have the chance to kiss me again. The night drifts away from us as it's filled with passion. The two of us finally fall asleep around five o'clock.

We're awaked to the sun shining through the spare bedroom window. It's now morning time and Sounni is still in the bed with me. My senses pick up Furrock's presence and then we can hear his footsteps. Thinking quickly I tell Sounni to act like she's picking up the room. I slowly open up the window and jump out. My first thought is to act as though I've been training. Furrock's presence once again makes it way to my senses. He picks up a rake and sets it up against his house and does a couple of more things acting as though he's doing something. My cheeks are as red as a Shogun blast, hoping that he will not mention a word of what transpired last night. He finally goes back into his house and after about twenty minutes I myself go back into the house. Jet pulls out a chair for me and puts a plate full of breakfast in front of me. Fresh pork sausage, pancakes and a Psychian treat fresh Pikna.

Pikna a treat held by Psychian's, a fruit that raises your stamina by just a little bit every time you eat it. This fruit gives you a little rush like steroids for humans.

The day goes by fast as we wait for the graduation party to start. About a little after five my parents arrive at Furrock's house. When they get off their horses I can't help myself, before my mind can compute I'm rushing towards my parents. The two of them greet me with the tightest hug they've ever given me in my life. Sorona, Sange and X arrive just as my parents do. After introductions are all said and done all of us go into Furrock's house and bring the tables outside to set up for the party. When the party is set up we all sit down for a speech from Furrock.

"I've known most of you kids for a long time and some of you I haven't known for very long at all". He starts. "I guess the point is congrats you five. My hopes is that for those with Shards in your blades, is that you stay on the side of good. Knowing at all times who your enemy is. Sometimes it's hard and other times you lose the people you know and love. Somehow though you find your way and hopefully that will be the same with the five of you...But for right now let's party".

All the people at the party stand up and clap at Furrock's speech. My feelings tell me that some of his speech had to do with his deceased wife. My suspicions are confirmed when I look over to Sounni and her eyes are filled with tears.

Sange puts in some music to a machine which spins a disc and music comes out of the speakers next to it.

Due to our powers abilities anything that is broken can be fixed. Batteries are of no use considering our powers will do just the same. By using computers we've figured out a lot from earth's past and devices used from that time.

Sounni and I are dancing when she pulls me close and ask if she and Sange can dance. Seeing as though him and X have no dates to dance with. Without question I let her go and sit down watching Sange and Sounni dance together. My father sits down at my table right beside me.

"She's a jewel son". My dad says.

"I know, why do you think we're together". I say

"Just remember you're a big target for the AU. So never let her be alone".

Reaching over to him we hug for a few seconds and then I take my place again dancing with Sounni. We're enjoying ourselves hugging, occasionally kissing and just listening to the music. Right before our little world of peace is turned to dread and despair.

Jet comes running out of the house yelling at the top of his lungs.

"What is it"? I ask.

"It's Rikki he's hurt, in the kitchen". Jet says hysterically.

When we walk into the kitchen there is a blonde haired man soaked in blood lying on the floor. Sounni lets out a scream of terror.

"X, Sange secure the perimeter". Furrock says. "How do you know him Jet"?

"We were both prisoners at Pokera he's the one who helped me escape". Jet says.

Furrock picks Rikki up and moves him into his bedroom. The sight of the blood soaking into his bed sheet sends Furrock into a trance. My father has to shake Furrock to get his friend out of the trance. They send us out of the room temporarily.

"Do you think he will make it"? X asks.

"I've seen him with worse than that". Jet says.

Watching Jet I notice that he is also in a trance now. My mouth cannot contain my question, I ask Sounni what happened to her father in his room.

"In that exact bed is where my mother was killed. My dad had returned to check up on my mother but when he called her name out there was no answer. When he walked into the room a man was standing over her with his blade through her heart. If my father had not come I would not be here either, as I was the man next target". Sounni says.

I walk over and hug her tight while she cries into my shoulder. After a few hours Furrock comes out and says that Rikki can be seen but he only wants to see Jet and I. When we walk into the room his body is bandaged almost head to toe. A few spots of his bandages are already stained with blood.

"His condition is critical but it looks as though he will make a full recovery. For right now keep it short and simple, stress on the brain and body is the last thing he needs". My dad says.

When we walk over to Rikki his eyes are closed, they slowly open up as we get closer.

"Jet you made it, and this must be Shinruga". Rikki barely mutters.

"Yes, I made it out and alive still". Jet says.

"I feel that you two are the only ones I can tell this to…You don't have much time. The warning I'm about to give you will save this town. Shiran cannot fall it's one of our Psychian's strongest town".

He can't finish his sentence so we give him some time to regain some strength. What he says though catches me completely off guard.

"The AU is coming with at least two hundred men…By tomorrow night". He says.

Hearing the news from what Rikki just told me I fall to my knees. Can it be possible the AU back in Shiran again? Are they going to reduce it to rubble? I won't let them this time it will be the AU who will die. Shiran will finally take it's vengeance on the AU.

CHAPTER 12

A DIFFERENT THREAT

It's now morning time and Jet, Sorona, Sange, X, Furrock and my father are all sitting in the living room. My father tells us to tell the others what Jet and I know. Jet and I take turns telling the others the information we now know. Silence falls over the room when we're done talking.

Tonight is the night that the AU comes to Shiran again. The warning Rikki gave us was pretty straight forward.

"Those pieces of dirt attacked are town once before reducing it to rubble. That isn't good enough for them"? Sorona rants.

My father slams his hand down, stands up and leaves the living room. When I find him in the kitchen he's standing over the sink with his head down.

"What is it dad"? I ask.

"Son, we left this town for one reason. That reason is so you would be safe but look what happened anyways. You just ended up back in Shiran anyways". He says.

Assuring my father that I will be safe, we go back into the living room with the others. Furrock and X are discussing what they should do to prevent casualties. It seems that Furrock and Sange have the same plan of action. Their plan is to get the word out to the rest of Shiran, without spreading word to the AU or any of their informants. We all agree that the AU should think that they have the upper hand, when they don't.

"All the mail must be checked to make sure". I say.

Furrock agrees anybody who refuses to show who or what they're mailing to, will be counted as a spy but not killed. They will be held prisoner until the invasion is over. The biggest part of our plan is to stay on the roof tops. Any Psychian's who come will take the roof tops to avoid being seen. The northern entrance will contain twenty Psychian's disguised as women. My father and the rest of us will be on Furrock's roof, waiting for our enemies. X and Sange will be stationed on the ground to help with the first assault. I go over to the window and look out at the beautiful town of Shiran. If you look closely enough you can see how colorful this town and its people. To think in just twelve hours nothing could be standing. A few more hours pass as the six of us sit there and discuss battle strategy. Sounni comes out of Rikki's room finally and says that he would like to see Jet and I again.

When we walk into the room his wounds look better and his bandages aren't blood soaked either. Sounni has washed all the dirt and blood off of him, he actually doesn't look to bad.

"Jet, is that you"? Rikki asks.

Jet grabs his hand and gives a little squeeze.

"Ah, it is you". Rikki says. "Your power has grown".

I'm not sure how he knows by that, something tells me it's a thing him and Jet made to greet each other.

"He's coming you know, he won't stop till he brings you back or he kills you".

"I know, trust me I've thought about it enough". Jet says.

Not being able to help myself, I blurt out my question and ask them whose coming.

"Shadow, he's my old guard. You're assigned groups in Pokera and there is one guard to your group who keeps you working". Jet says. "Mine and Rikki's guard was a Psychian named Shadow. Whenever someone escapes it is that guard's responsibility to track their slaves down. I'm surprised he hasn't already found me".

"It's because you didn't even know where you were going. Having no knowledge of your hometown or family, that makes it harder to track you down". Rikki explains.

"Now that I've been traveling with you and making marks all over cities and the school he will surely be upon us soon".

"Probably didn't help that he hit me in a place that I would bleed profusely. By doing so I made a trail right to Shiran". Rikki says.

"Don't worry about it Shadow already knew where you were from. So it's not your fault". I say.

The idea of it seems to comfort Rikki a little bit, enough to where he actually sits up in bed. His wounds seem to be healing faster than a normal Psychian's rate. Asking Jet about it he explains his theory to me. If you live your whole life being tortured and whipped you learn to heal faster and pain is a little more bearable.

After a few more minutes Rikki lays back down on the bed, he asks us to leave so he can take a nap. When we return to the living room everyone is gone. Sounni tells us that they are outside. Outside everyone is partnered up and training but not hard enough to use any energy, seeing as we will need it for the battle tonight. I go back into the house to get a drink but when I do Sounni is in the kitchen cleaning up the rest of the stuff from the party. She tells me that there is some Pikna juice in the fridge.

"I just prepared it today". She says.

Something on her face gives me a clue something's wrong. After pouring my drink I pull her closer to me and give her a big kiss. As we sit there kissing my world becomes hers and hers to mine. I help her clean the room of all the cups and plates. Finally I can't contain myself and I ask her what's wrong.

"I don't even know why I'm cleaning this place, it might all get destroyed anyways".

A few more minutes go by and I join my friends and family outside. My father directs Jet to train with me.

"Listen closely kids human soldiers main weapon is his gun. In this exercise your partner will shoot a gun at you, the bullet will be aimed beside you. This will help you judge how far away the gun will be fired by listening closely". My father explains.

In a way he's always been a teacher, he's even been asked to be one. He turned the offers down though after he caught the Elemenka gems he figured his work was done. I guess he figured that since he had a family and no one after him, there was any reason to fight or get involved with anything anymore.

"If you disarm an AU's gun they are almost powerless but beware they have no respect for the word honor". He goes on.

In the middle of our training Septh comes to Furrock's house. We're all surprised when he knows of the troop of units coming to Shiran. He asks us all if we would like his help. We immediately answer his question with a huge yes.

Septh may only be about twenty years old but he has more strength than mine and Sounni's dad put together. His power feels weird compared to most Psychian's, when I feel out other Psychian's power my body is fine. His though makes a sickly feel to my stomach, people say it's because of how much power he possess.

Septh asks my father if he could borrow me for a little bit. At first he tells Septh no but I assure him that everything will be fine. We walk a little bit heading northeast into town. I ask him what we're doing and where we're going. He takes me behind a house next to the woods and removes a piece of plywood from the trees. When he does I notice the trees are scorched and broke down.

"What happened"? I ask.

"Feel he's in that direction". He says.

I close my eyes and feel for energy in the direction he's pointed. When my energy finally feels it I'm forced to sink to my knees. An image goes in my head of red eyes and a ripped up red cloak. The persons face is distorted and weird looking.

"What was that"?

"His name is Warlord, head of the mutant's son. His father is the head of the mutants and they're now helping Kita and the AU". Septh says.

Mutants created before we Psychian's were born. They were left scarred and separated from their former selves and people. They hide underground occasionally coming up to steal food and other stuff. They are also much different from the creatures that were under Ikeya's school. They don't eat Psychian's or people and have powers like us Psychian's.

"He stole a blade and somehow transported here but had no sheath so the blade burned the ground and destroyed the trees". Septh explains.

"What does this have to with me"? I ask.

"Because he could be another possible threat, along with Kita and the AU". He says.

My mind starts racing at the thought of having to face someone else with immense power. Septh tells me that I should get back to my friends. He will take a patrol of the city to make sure he can't see the AU.

As I walk back it's nearing dusk now and in about an hour or so it should be nighttime. When I return to my friends my father pulls me to a side of the house that no one can hear us talking.

"Son, what did he talk to you about I need to know".

"He told me of a mutant with extraordinary powers and he's working with Kita and the AU". I say.

My father pulls out a piece of paper and hands it to me. When I take a look at the paper I can see that it's a picture. The picture contains Septh standing over a guy with his Septh's blade in his chest. There is also two other people in the photo.

"On that picture you can see Septh right there. The other person with him is a known AU subordinate and if you look closely enough you can see".

"Ikeya"! I cut him off. "But who's the guy who they killed"?

My father turns and looks the other way. He asks me if I can remember my uncle who died in the first attack on Shiran. Searching back to my memories I can make out a clear distinct picture of him.

Psychian's have the ability to retrieve memories even of when they were only two years of age. It's like a photographic memory times ten fol.

"You remember his son Travor"?

"Not really all that much". I say.

My father goes on to tell me that the one with sword in his chest is my cousin. He also informs me that Septh is the one that stabbed him. Asking who the AU subordinate is my father can offer no answer. He only says nothing with tears in his eyes. He finally says something but all he does say is to get some sleep before the AU arrive. Walking back to Furrock's house, how can I think of sleep when I know Septh has betrayed all of us? How can my father act so casual around him? When I get into the house I plop onto the couch and close my eyes and set a mental alarm for to sleep for a few hours.

A few hours go by with no nightmares for once. When I wake up from my slumber Sounni is lying in front of me. The sun is about five minutes from being covered by the horizon. Shrugging Sounni's shoulders she wakes up instantly. I remind her to get to the basement, when we get down there she grabs my face and plants her lips to mine. Pushing her into the room she mutters three words I will always hold dear to my heart.

"I love you too". I respond back.

After she's inside the door I push it shut and seal it with my energy. Running up the stairs and out the door to the roof, I rejoin my friends and family. We all crouch down and wait for the AU. My father instructs us to keep low and to watch each other's back. The city keeps its lights on to make it appear as nothing is out of the ordinary. Ahead I can see several factions of Psychian's on other rooftops. The wall that surrounds Shiran which is usually lit up, is now dimmed. For some reason the lights around the edge of town go dim and the center glows even brighter. I scoot closer to my father to ask what is going on.

"We put out word that Shiran is going to be having a festival". He whispers. "That way the AU will think our defenses will be even lower than usual".

No doubt his idea given the way he presents the lie.

"What is that"? Jet whispers.

A Psychian's vision is almost just as good at night as it is in the day.

My dad moves over by Jet who's about to fire a blast. He ask Jet to wait and look closer, after a few seconds we can all see that it's a deer. Thirty minutes go by watching for our enemy until Furrock sees something.

"At my three and twelve, two groups inbound". He says.

When I look over to our three I can see them, forty or more dressed in full body armor guns pointed in the air. It has been seven years and this time we got the upper hand. The AU has arrived and it's now time for Shiran to take its vengeance.

CHAPTER 13

ATTACKED AGAIN

Night One

As the AU storm into the city our troops position themselves to attack. To the northeast there is a small explosion from a frag grenade, signaling that the fighting has started. A troop of about twenty AU units are right below us. My father and I swoop down landing on top of two and shooting the others with our energy blast. One comes from behind me with a sword but I simply duck, flipping him over my shoulder I kick him in the face knocking him out. X and Furrock join the fight when my father and I are surrounded. With their help we manage to take out the first group with ease. My father commands Jet, Sorona, X, Sange and I to go west and dispatch our enemies. He reminds us not to kill unless we absolutely have no choice.

When we arrive it's a blood bath as our fellow brethren are being killed off as if they're cattle. X and I fire blasts of energy at the AU scum. Jet turns into his Phercon form and attacks. Their numbers dwindle down as the five of us unleash an onslaught of attacks on the AU. X is slashing at one of his opponents when another sneaks behind him. I reach in my bag and throw a ninja star. It strikes my target in his temple, the ground in front of raises up. When I look over Sange has a smirk on his face. He points his finger to my twelve. Closing my eyes I can now hear the snipers firing their silenced guns above us. The five of us make shields of earth to cover ourselves.

"I got this". I yell.

Changing into Kimoshiran form I use the K-gateway (Kimoshiran Gateway) technique to appear behind the snipers. Their surprised but their quick reflexes make them no easy opponent. I draw my sword deflecting their bullets away from myself. They soon overwhelm me though and about knock me off of the roof. X though comes to my rescue drawing a couple of the snipers fire. I lay waste to the two still firing at me, cutting them in half. The third and fourth one I hit with the bottom of my sword, only knocking them out.

"Shinruga, we could use your help down here". X yells.

Rejoining my friends on the ground we soon are surrounded by AU insurgents. I change back into Psychian warrior form and tell my friends to make four shields to enclose the five of us. Using my energy I make an enormous Implosion box around the AU and the five of us. By squeezing my hand into a fist the box shrinks, when it touches the first AU guard the box explodes. Smoke fills the area and when it dissipates there are only dead bodies left. The five of us check around and find a startling surprise.

"The Psychian bodies they were kids". Sorona says.

"They look to be about ten or eleven years old". X remarks.

We have little time to look as the explosions are getting closer to our area. The five of us take to the roofs and wait for our enemies. I caution the team to duck as our enemies come into the plaza. As we're crouched down I notice Jet losing his footing. He falls in between two buildings and in seconds the AU have their guns focused on his location. We wait for the opportune moment and strike, creating a plaza of death. Jet turns into his Phercon form once again as the four of us fire blasts at the other enemies. The fighting has stopped but I catch an AU soldier out of the corner of my eye. Sange realizes this before I do and chucks his sword; the blade strikes the soldier in the head.

"All this bloodshed and for what"! Sange yells.

"Our freedom and lives"! X says.

Sange walks over and pulls the blade out the soldiers head. Hearing more explosions to the east we press on, leaving the bodies of the AU and our Psychian brothers and sisters behind. The town of Shiran a few hours ago so beautiful now burned and battle scarred, full of bodies and blood.

When we get closer to the explosions my father appears out of nowhere and pushes me to the side. An RPG bullet is coming straight in his direction. He puts energy in his hand when the RPG gets close to him he captures it in the energy and shoots it back at our opponent.

"How did everything go in the west quadrant"? He asks.

We relay the grim news to my father. Furrock soon joins our group with an energy wolf at his side. Soon more insurgents are coming our way but my father and Furrock only take a few seconds to dispatch the troop of AU. The five of us are mesmerized as they seem to be gods. After the two of them dispose of our enemies we all take cover behind a destroyed building wall. As we're sitting there resting another one of Furrock's energy wolf approaches. The wolf turns sideways and in the middle of its stomach an image of a Psychian appears.

"Master Furrock this is Lao in the south quadrant we're taking extreme fire and need assistance. The western and eastern sections are under control. If we lose the southern part of Shiran there will be critical losses".

The image disappears and the wolf goes back to where it came from.

"Ok, here's what we will do. Since we haven't heard anything from the northern section Furrock you X, and Sange go to the north. Shinruga, Sorona, Jet and I will go to the South". My dad says.

Before we depart my father and Furrock shake hands and hit their shoulders to each others. Their friendship runs thicker than blood.

Down the road a little ways there is something blocking our way. It looks as to be some kind of metal machine that can move.

My father warns us not to stay in one spot for more than a few seconds. We soon learn why a small thin blast comes out of a gun mounted on its shoulder.

"Shinsaga, we need to make some kind of diversion". Jet yells.

"Agreed"!

Sorona and I run in from side to side to confuse the hunk of metal. The machine begins firing randomly hoping to hit one of us. Unfortunately it does, as Jet is trying to launch an energy blast the machine fires one of its lasers skinning the top of his right shoulder. The robot moves in closer to finish Jet but my father jumps on its back, grabbing the gun pointing at the robots head. The bucket of bolts crashes to the ground with a gaping hole in its head. Sorona runs over to Jet applying energy to his wound in an attempt to heal it.

The sound of another explosion towards the south sends us running back to into harm's way. When we arrive to the rendezvous point our brethren is under heavy fire.

"Where's Lao"? My father asks.

"Dead sir, he took a bullet to the head".

"You get your wounded out of here whoever can fight keep them here". He orders.

For the Psychian's still able to fight he commands them to try and get to higher ground. When I peak my head up to see our enemies there's nothing. The shooting has disappeared along with our enemies. We carefully stalk to where the firing was coming from.

"An automated Gatling gun. There around they wouldn't leave something that could later be used against them". The first lieutenant says in anger.

"All right spread out men and watch your backs". My dad commands.

Pulling out my sword with my right hand and filling my left with energy, I creep into an alley way. While I'm in the alley way I can see them about forty AU soldiers charging at me. I yell out for my fellow companions to help. They begin firing energy blasts at the AU but one of them tackles me to the ground. Puts his gun around my throat and begins choking me.

My only thought is that I'm going to die that no matter which way I move, his strength will overpower mine. That's when I can see it Furrock's energy wolf, jumping over me and ripping out my enemies throat. My father grabs me up by the arm and orders me to keep fighting. We stand back to back swords drawn and waiting for our enemies to shoot us down.

"Fire"! Yells out the AU soldiers superior.

When he does we simply deflect their bullets back at them with our swords. Looking around most of the AU soldiers is dead. Their superior however is not, Sorona walks over to him and finishes him.

"These scum I wish they'd all die". She says.

"Easy Sorona, no unnecessary killing". My father reminds her.

Furrock's energy wolf walks by us once again, with a sketchy message from Furrock himself.

"My friend it's been reported from the outer wall, that another one hundred and fifty AU soldiers have been spotted". Furrock relays. "This looks like it might go on for a couple of days...M".

The message cuts out as an RPG goes by Furrock's head.

"Is he dead"? Jet asks.

My father reminds Jet that the energy wolf has not disappeared, so Furrock is still alive.

"But he could be hurt badly, so we should make haste". Sorona points out.

We run in the direction of our fallen comrade as we hope for the best. The sun is now coming up over the horizon as it marks the second fight for all of Shiran. I pray that this glorious city defenses can hold till we scare off our enemies.

Day One

When we get to where the message was recorded at, there is only rubble and death. My father tells us to feel for Furrock's energy, after a few seconds Jet locates him. He's hiding under a board propped up so you can barely see into it. Jet carefully pulls him out from under his hiding place. The right side of his jacket is burned and shredded. His skin is dark red from the heat. Sorona runs over to tend to his wounds.

"There first degree burns but he should be ok". She says.

"Soldiers are still in the area. They're using some type of device to communicate, a walky talky I think". Furrock mutters.

"Keep him awake and heal him at the same time if his energy wolf are gone the AU will have this place in a matter of hours". My father remarks.

Just as he's finished with his sentence we're attacked by a troop of AU. My father yells for us to take cover. Sorona crawls under the boards with Furrock.

"All of you use your energy to create a grenade, focus your energy into the middle of your hand for three seconds and chuck it". My father commands.

When we throw our grenades the AU soldiers duck for cover. In the middle of our fight one of Furrock's energy wolfs gets in front of me. One of our commander's faces appears, he asks for my dad but instead I say he's too busy and take over. The commander tells me that they are taking to heavy of fire to even move. Thinking for a few seconds I suggest that they put their swords into the ground and push it into the earth in front of their enemies to deflect their bullets back at them. He thinks about it for a second and says he'll give it a try. Furrock's wolf goes away and I return to the fight at hand. My father and Jet have moved up to another house to take cover. The wolf that had appeared in front me a few minutes ago is now up by my father. He looks back at me and tells me to advance up to his position.

"General, Shinsaga your sons plan worked out perfectly. The southeast division of Shiran is now clear". Says the commander.

"Good to hear commander now get your men to the north outer wall. We're taking heavy fire and short on troops". He commands.

"Where's X and Sange at"? I ask.

"That's a good question". He says.

The AU soldiers take position behind the destroyed library. From what we can see they have set up two Gatling guns. Aiming at precise parts of the destroyed house we're in the whole place starts falling apart. We jump to our sides to avoid being crushed by the building but find ourselves outside in our targets sights.

We hear the leader of the AU soldiers yell out to fire. As the bullets get closer my father holds me and hopes that I will be shielded. The bullets are in front of us now and we think we're done for when a wall of rock shields us. X and Sange jump in front of us, they send the wall of earth at the AU. Soon energy rain down upon us. We move out of the way so we won't be hit by the blasts. We look around for our attacker but no luck.

"That was definitely Psychian energy". X says.

'It's him Shadow". Jet says. "That's his sign to let you know he's around".

We press on slashing our enemies down but another hundred AU soldiers arrive. We're outnumbered by a lot and no chance at winning. That's when they arrive the commander we talked to in Furrock's wolf.

"Sir, it's been reported that another two hundred troops have entered the city".

"Sure glad you came". My dad replies. "We have a couple of Psychian traitors on our hands".

Our last remaining troops try to fend off the few dozen left. We have our enemies backed up against the wall when my sight suddenly goes blurry and my head is ringing. Luckily I put up a shield to defend myself from harm and so the entire troop.

"A flash bang men". Says my father.

He asks Sorona to come out of her hiding place. Furrock is lifted out as well and he looks a lot better, Sorona's healing abilities out match any of us other Psychian's.

"Where were you two at"? My dad asks.

"We got pinned down in the northeast region". X's quick to answer.

My father gives X a weird look seeing as he's so quick to answer the question. Furrock is now able to stand and checks in with all of his wolves. If it wasn't for his wolves I don't think things would be going as smooth in this war. One of the commanders in the southeast is being pinned down by a skirmish of AU soldiers. Heading towards the direction that we're going we run into a small group of Psychian's.

Their faces I can still remember them scared but ready to fight. Most of their team is wounded, shot in the arm. As we're running one of our Psychian comrades falls to the ground.

"Leave him, he's dead". My father commands. "I felt his power slipping from his as we were running".

Could my father's senses be that great, that even in the heat of battle and running he can feel energies?

After a few minutes of running we stop to grab something to eat. We find refuge in a home and move boards to make it look as though it is abandoned. Something about the house looks familiar and then I realize it's our old house. My father must know it to because he hardly says a thing the whole meal. Memories fill back into my head, of me being a child and playing with my mom and dad. Sorona has to shrug my shoulder to snap me out of my hallucination.

Our troop marches forward to defend the city against its intruders. As the sun sets we get closer to the location where are brethren is being pinned down. When we get to the location most of our men is dead. We take cover with the few surviving Psychian troops.

"What happened here solider"? My father asks.

"We were fine until two Psychian's showed up. I figured they were friendly but when we turned our backs they started attacking". He says.

He looks frightened his eyes are going nuts as they look in every direction. It's now turning to night time slowly and we wait for the Psychian bogeys to return. A few hours later I can hear some rustling in the broken down house to my left. Jet and I explore the house, at first nothing happens. In a second an AU soldier jumps out at me, I kick him in the head knocking him to the ground. Jet gets surprised by two men and easily handles them. Thanks to his quick reflexes he deflects another attacker's kunai.

"I was wondering when you'd find me". Jet says.

"You knew I would come". The voice says.

From a Shadow a Psychian appears and another to his right. Now on guard Jet identifies the other assailant as Gringold his partner in evil. The first of the two is Shadow his torturer of Pokera.

"Jet, prisoner I-200 last name unknown. I have a warrant to bring you back or to kill you on sight". Shadow says.

They stare each other down for a few minutes and then attack. Gringold charges at Jet as well but I step into harm's way. I block his kunai from going into Jet's head.

My father finally figures out our location. After a few minutes another troop of AU soldiers come marching into the plaza. My father and X uses their energy to swing a broken roof down to block us while they duck for cover.

Gringold and I are in a standoff, his muscles are rippling out of his body. His eyes are dark with evil and as if he's heartless. There are broken blades absorbed into his body that went to deep to retrieve. Most likely from all the fights he's been in. He charges again but I learn of what all the blades in his body are for. They're an attack the blades stick out of his body, blood starts pouring out of his wounds.

"What the hell"? I ask.

How am I supposed to fight an enemy I can't touch? Quickly jumping out of his direction I think over a strategy. The blood pouring out of his wounds will take its toll eventually he will have to stop using this fatal attack or else he will bleed to death. Moving backwards my feet are stopped suddenly by something hard. Directly behind me there is a fence of sword blades sticking out of the ground.

"Trying to buy enough time till I bleed to death"? He asks. "Try something new kid, I've been around the block a bit more than you have".

He charges a few more times trying to impale me but fortunately no success. Angry he extends the blades out of his body even further. The blood begins to pour faster now but when he does ram there will be no safe spot in this fenced area. When he charges I pull out a few shurikens and throw them but they do no good. He's only a few feet away from impaling me when a red dot appears in the middle of his head. A bullet zooms by my head, striking Gringold directly between his eyes. Looking back I can see my father on the ground with a gun resting on his shoulders.

"Good shot". I yell.

He nods and commands the troop to finish the job. Rushing over to watch Jet he is nowhere to be found. As I listen closer my ears pick up faint grunting sounds. A story up Jet and Shadow are duking it out still. My father soon joins me at my side, to view the fight. It's now a concept of the former slave defeating his owner. This is the day Jet has dreamed of for a while now to take his revenge and finish off the one who mistreated him all those years. The rest of the troop come from below and relay the good news to my father.

"Sir, master Furrock's wolves have all come back. They all report the same the AU insurgents have been killed and or scared off".

"You hear that Shadow, it's over. You're the only one still fighting, give up now". My father demands.

Shadow keeps fighting with Jet and ignores my dad's command. Jet's opponent disappears into a shadow but Jet turns into Phercon form. He opens his mouth and blast the surrounding area.

"He's wasting energy". I say.

My father tells me to look closer at Jet's strategy. After a few seconds my brain finally figures it out, about half of this room is made of wood and now it's on fire. Without any shadows to hide in Jet's opponent appears instantly.

Shadow charges but Jet simply throws his opponent off of him and stomps on his chest again and again.

"I give up". Shadow yells. "Kill me then Jet, it's what you've always wanted isn't it…DO IT".

Jet unsheathes his sword and holds it high up in the air. My thoughts race as he holds that sword up, is he really going to do it, would he kill him for revenge? Right when I think Jet's going to take his revenge he puts his sword back into its sheathe.

"I can't do it". Jet says.

"Then you're still weak you fool". Shadow rants.

Jet turns and starts walking away from his beaten opponent. Shadow stands up and starts glowing white a sign that he's using his life energy. He extends his arms out and fires the glowing white energy at Jet. Before Jet has any time to react my father appears in front of the blast with his hand full of energy. He walks closer to Shadow, who only adds more energy to his surprise blast. I yell out as my father is only a few feet from Shadow.

"NO, DIE SHINSAGA"! Shadow yells.

As my father inches closer I can see the energy consume his opponent, the blast starts disintegrating his skin. Soon there is nothing left of Shadow as the blast has completely obliterated him into dust.

I run to my father to make sure that he is all right.

"Yeah, burned my hand a little that's all". He says.

As we stand there on top of the building it reminds us of how lucky we are to have each other. Also to know that Shiran is now safe warms our hearts a little. Now we look forward for our days to help each other rebuild this proud city. Shiran was finally able to claim it's vengeance on the AU. Somewhere I would hope Kita is banging his fist against the wall filled with anger.

CHAPTER 14

REBUILDING

Shiran is a mess, nearly three quarters of the city is either burned or tore down. Thanks to Rikki's warning though there is few causalities.

I'm now in Furrock's house again prepared to strike if anyone is to sneak up on me. My sword drawn I make my way to the basement. From all directions I can see no one, so I go deeper into the basement. Finally my body makes it to the door where I sealed Sounni, to make sure she stayed safe during the war. Using my energy I unseal the door it gently opens up.

"Is it over"? She asks.

"Yeah, we drove them off and thanks to your cousins warning there was few casualties". I say.

"Is everyone all right"?

"Pretty much, your father got a little banged up and so did Jet".

Sadness befalls her face upon hearing the news about her father. She asks me where he is being treated at. Using my index finger I point to the upstairs. She bolts up the stairs to go see her father. When Sounni see Furrock she collapses on top his chest and starts crying. Furrock groans a little as she is lying on top of him. My father nudges me to get out of the room. He tells me to give the two of them a little time together. We go outside and climb to the roof to look at the damage to Shiran.

"You see the western part of town son"? My father asks.

"Yeah, that's what it looked like all those years ago". I say.

"Do you still miss her"? He asks.

The fact that he asked about my sister surprises me, seeing as though he never talks about his daughter. He was so proud of her and when she left it hurt him so bad. My father loved his daughter so much, after she left he fell apart for some time. Furrock came to visit every other weekend so he would start feeling better. Around the time I was seven he focused his attention on me. Giving me the same training she endured even though I couldn't do half as good. He stops talking and jumps off of the roof.

"Sir, we need some help in the western division, the weather predicts rain tonight and half of our people are without shelter of any kind".

"I will get my sons friends together to help and then we will be there in a few". Dad says.

We go into the house and gather up the rest of our friends. On the way to the western region my eyes catch a person standing in his kitchen. Looking closely I notice that the support beams are about to give way. I hop off of my blade and send a pillar of earth from the ground to hold up the rest of his house.

"Quick thinking son"! My father remarks.

When we arrive at the rendezvous point the place is full of bodies and battle scars. There is body upon body of AU soldiers lying in the street. There are also a few Psychian bodies full of bullet wounds. One of them is actually alive but in critical condition. My father makes an assessment of his wounds.

"He can't survive, his wounds are too great. I give him another few hours".

"Master Shinsaga, can you take my life but make it an honorable death". The Psychian begs.

My father kneels over the dying Psychian and pulls out his sword. He places the blade up to the Psychian's heart and with one fluent motion they stab his heart together. The Psychian's eyes go dark and my father closes his eyelids.

"You see Shinruga, this is what is going on in every town. Do you see how many innocent people are dying, they won't stop till we're all dead. If you are to become the Triple Psychian it is your responsibility to end the war". My father says.

He yells this loud enough for all the Psychian's around him. We go back to work fixing the surrounding buildings and putting out fires. By the end of the day the western region looks almost as if nothing happened. We're then called to the southern part of Shiran for help, seems as though ten or so AU troops were hiding in an abandoned building. We get there a few minutes later and our Psychian comrades are still taking heavy fire.

"Sir, there placed in spots that our energy can't sneak up on them". The commander yells. "They also have two Gatling guns placed on the top of the building".

My father sits down for a few seconds to think of a strategy but he has no luck. Under my feet a spout of water bursts up.

"Hey, wait a minute where do the pipes for this water lead to"? I ask.

"Up through that building I'm pretty sure". The commander answers.

Using my energy I block the water from coming or going.

"What is your kid doing"? Asks the commander.

My father directs their attention to the building with our enemies. With my energy feeding into the pipe to stop the water the pressure begins to rise until the water breaks through the pipes and floods all the floors of the abandoned building. Most of the Au soldiers can't get a grip and hang from the building. My reflexes try to kick in but my father holds me back. He holds the blade of his sword out and the automated Gatling gun shoots a few rounds. We can hear the AU soldiers calling out for help but with no way to save them, they fall to their death. With no way to destroy the Gatling guns we're about to leave. That's when a beam of energy strikes the top of the building. Half of the building top is reduced to rubble and the Gatling guns are destroyed.

"Well that took quite a bit of energy to destroy". A voice says.

A figure soon lurks into our view, it's Septh. He's out of breath and holding two AU soldiers in his hands.

"Picked up these two stragglers back a little ways". He says.

My dad and I are both on edge once we realize that it's Septh. Septh ask my father is he would like the honor of killing the soldiers. He declines his offer and tries to reason with Septh.

"No unnecessary killing Hiraski's orders". My father tells him.

"I'm not Hiraski's lap dog". Septh says in anger.

I can see the AU soldier's faces pale and scared. Septh unsheathes his blade and is about to slice their heads off but I'm quick to react as our blades collide.

"What the, you foolish boy they're our enemies".

He pushes his blade off of mine and shoots a couple of blast of energy at me. Using my quick reflexes I position my blade back into the direction of his blade. Septh powers up his immense power till I slide backwards away from him.

"I am the Golden child stronger than any normal Psychian, second to the Triple Psychian no one can defeat me. If anyone is to get in my way or kill my kind they'll be the ones with their heads cut off". He yells.

"Son stay back you can't win he's too strong". My father yells.

Septh finally powers down but I heed my father's warning and stay back this time. He once again pulls his sword out but before we can blink our eyes Septh's blade claims his victim's throats.

Our troop stays on guard as Septh walks towards me. He warns that if I ever get in his path again my head won't be attached to my neck. He surrounds himself with energy and jumps a hundred feet from our location. Is his energy that incredible that he can almost fly?

My father walks towards the dead bodies and looks closely at them. He shakes his head in disappointment at this senseless killing.

"My men, what you just witnessed never happened. If you can help yourself try not to kill unless you have to. These men could have been persuaded not to kill but now we will never know". My father preaches.

Our troop starts leaving to another location to help. I stay behind with my father to bury the bodies of the two soldiers.

"Why did you say to them that this never happened"? I ask.

"Because we can't do nothing about it son, Septh is the only Psychian that doesn't have to take orders. He's stronger than any of us, his powers exceed mine and Furrock's both". He says.

"What do you mean take orders"? I ask.

"All the Psychian's here are following orders even I. From your future master…Hiraski. His blood is the same blood that flowed through the past Triple Psychian. Until the new Triple Psychian appears he is the Psychian who controls the actions of this war. Most don't question him because so far every plan he's put into plan has resulted in success. He's not our master or our king but he's done well enough so far, best to keep listening to him". He explains.

I nod in approval and go about the day helping in the effort to clean up the city. When it gets close to night I head back to Furrock's house. There is a pot of stew on the stove I go to take a bite but Sounni slaps my hand out of the way. She wraps her arms around my body and squeezes me till I give her a kiss.

"Well how'd it go out there"? She asks.

Sitting down on the chair I tell her of Septh and what my father had told me. She puts a bowl of soup down in front of me; it's delicious full of spices and fried pork. After all of the work today the soup makes me feel full and warm. When I finish my soup we go into the living room and sit down on the couch. We hold each other tightly as if it will be the last time. Furrock soon comes out of his room holding his side and groaning every time he moves. He watches us for a few seconds and then goes into the kitchen and gets a bite to eat or so I thought.

"Hey, Shinruga"! Furrock says.

My senses pick up someone hovering over me; it's Furrock with a blade pointing down on me. Of course I jump halfway across the room at his prank. He goes down the hallway laughing the whole way at the success of his prank.

"Dad, I'm going to kill you myself"? Sounni yells.

"Will he ever stop that stuff"? I say aloud.

She shakes her head and tells me a few stories of how our dads use to play pranks on each other all the time. For some reason unbeknownst to her I'm the only one he's done it to since her mom died. We stay up for another hour or so and then go off into the bedroom. Furrock comes in a little bit later, he says goodnight and tells me the others all made it there safely. Showing no anger at the two of us sleeping in the same bed we snuggle closer and both drift off to sleep.

The next day Sounni and I wake up to the smell of breakfast cooking. When we enter the kitchen X is cooking breakfast for everybody.

"Morning love birds". He says. "Furrock and Shinsaga gave us a day off because of how much work we've done all this week".

After we're finished with breakfast we join my father and Jet outside. X and Furrock join us a few minutes later after they've finished eating. Jet and my father are doing a little bit of sparring. Furrock tells X and I to join them to fight my father. Sounni and Sorona who has now joined us are sitting on the deck sipping on some tea.

"Come on let's see if you three have any fighting skills at all"? My dad boasts.

Not too long after we start sparring we knock my dad on his butt. He starts laughing but trips all three of us. We can hear Sounni and Sorona laughing at our expense. The three of us soon start overpowering my dad but not too long after we do Furrock jumps into the battle. His attacks are flawless and fighting the two of them we soon become overpowered.

Soon Sorona also jumps into the fray she doesn't only fight but helps the old people. I join Sounni on the porch to watch the fight.

"Where's Sange"? I ask her.

"Out helping some more he was sick yesterday, so he's making up for lost time". She says.

As it gets closer to dinner we all head out to Bickery's. We meet Sange on the way there, who reports that the whole city has been temporarily fixed for now. Being the heroes of Shiran the waiter tells us that our meal is on the house. Bickery's our favorite restaurant, where the food will make you want to stay there forever. We enjoy our time together eating and laughing knowing that we have earned this day and that for a little while we're safe.

CHAPTER 15

A NEW FOE

We wake up the next day with reports from our troops that most of Shiran's buildings have been repaired. The total death toll of Psychian's and humans alike comes to about fifty. Rikki's warning saved a lot of lives in that battle. Rikki himself is finally healing at a regular rate, he can even walk around for about an hour before he has to sit down and rest.

Late in the morning there is a knock at the door. When the door opens Shokon is standing there with a smirk on his face.

"Been a while Shinruga". Shokon says.

"Yeah, no kidding"! I say.

I invite him into the house to sit down for a drink. Always noticing the little things I notice that when he sits down it's unnatural. I can't help myself so I ask him what happened to his leg. Shokon pulls up his pant leg and reveals a cut. Asking him where he got it, he shrugs his shoulder and tells us the usual. He explains that he ran into a small cache of AU soldiers carrying Psychian prisoners.

"Heard about this town and how you seven are the heroes of Shiran". He says. "Man wish I was here to help, one have been a blast".

"Yeah, we definitely could have used you, being that you used to be AU yourself". X says walking into the kitchen.

"I've changed haven't been a part for quite a while now. You yourself were a big candidate for being recruited". Shokon snaps back.

Reminding the two of them whose house this is they both back down. Shokon goes on to tell us that every AU soldier is looking for the bounty on our heads. From his and X's little ranting session I can feel that his power has increased a good size. Feeling bad for yelling X makes him some breakfast and after he is done we go outside to look at Furrock's property.

"It's a beautiful house and city. How much do you love her"? He asks.

"Sounni, a lot"! I say.

We walk around the property for a little while longer until the sun has an hour or so before it settles. Heading back to the house my senses pick up an attack behind me. Pushing Shokon to the side we barely avoid the attack. When I turn around there is a man in a red hooded cape and his eyes are glowing deep red.

"Warlord"! I say.

His power far exceeds my own but I power up to my maximum. Shokon must also sense his power level because he also powers up as well. Soon everyone comes out of the house but for some reason my father and Furrock is nowhere to be found.

"Good but those few puny powers won't be able to do nothing". Warlord says.

He takes his hood of off his head, his eyes still glowing red. His hair is spiked up and his ears look as a creature from another planet. His clothes only cover about half of his body. His eyes have markings on them that go halfway down his cheeks.

Sorona and Sange charge but it only takes a few seconds for Warlord to knock them to the ground. X and Shokon charge at him as well and Warlord does the same. Now it's just me and him, he charges and he's too quick for me to even see. The thing I feel is pain as his fist connects with my gut. I fall to the ground begging for air to reach my lungs. He stands me up and takes a step back he charges up an attack in his hands that is a ball. When I look closer into it I can see me and the surrounding area. He fires his attack I quickly summon an Electric Psych Ball to defend the attack. The attack sends me back grinding on the ground; using the sparks on the ground I add electricity to the EPB to increase its power. Soon I'm against Furrock's kitchen wall and power of Warlord's attack is increasing. Using what little energy I have

I shield myself from the blast when it explodes. The explosion sends me crashing through Furrock's kitchen wall.

"Hey, babe how you doing"? I say to Sounni.

She rushes over to help me up but I tell her to go wake up our dads. Sounni zooms down the hall to our father's rooms. They come out wiping the sleep off of their eyes.

"What'd you do to my kitchen kid"? Furrock asks.

Warlord comes walking into the kitchen, staring down my dad and Furrock.

"A mutant"! They say at the same time.

"Furrock and Shinsaga, nice to see you again"! Warlord says.

"How's the old man doing"? My dad asks.

He assures them that he's fine now that he's made a full recovery since their fight. Hearing this makes a lot of questions come to mind. How do the three of them know each other? Who is Warlord's father and when did they fight?

My father and Furrock get into fighting position. Warlord charges at them unlike us the two of them can hold their own. As the fight goes on their power begins to surge and fire off at random. Fearing for Sounni's life being that she's is human I take action. When Warlord's distracted enough I jump up kicking him to the head, the attack sends him flying back outside onto the ground. The three of us is on guard when we walk outside to confront our enemy once more. Our other five friends join us as well they look a little ruffed up from their encounter with Warlord. While we wait my father and Furrock give me what energy they can, so that I may heal. Warlord finally stands up and stares the eight of us down surrounding him.

"Now"! My father yells.

The eight of us all fire a blast of energy at our opponent, they collide in the middle. None of us can see our opponent in the middle. His presence is above us, when we look he is firing that same attack down on us. Instead of continuing to fire our blast we scramble to find safety. The explosion makes a crater in the ground the size of a house.

The eight of us are bruised and beaten but we continue to fight. Soon we begin to overpower Warlord but we realize his full power, he rises to a level that hurts our stomachs. Just when we think we're done a figure comes from the shadows in a cloak and a round straw hat and a pair of kunai at his side. The eight of us sit there confused as Warlord let's his guard down and stares at the man. Before our eyes can fathom what happened the figure is choking Warlord. He soon lets him go and backs up a few feet.

"Who is that"? My dad asks.

He orders the seven of us to get by his side and me behind everyone. Just like my K-Gateway technique Warlord goes up in a flash of red lightning into a red swirling portal.

"I'll be back, Shinruga and next time you won't be so lucky". Warlord assures me.

The man in the cloak begins walking down the street from where he came. Curiously I follow him but when I take the same corner he does the man is gone. Looking in all directions I cannot see him but then there is a voice.

"Shinruga, we will soon meet and when we do I will improve your power by ten times the amount". He says.

Asking when I will see him, I wait for a response but no response ever comes. I tread my way back to the house and into the living room. Furrock is ranting about how he just fixed the kitchen and it's destroyed again. Standing up Shokon announces that he has rented a place not far from here and will return in the morning. Sange and Sorona also leave out to go home. He simply raises a slab of earth and uses a few boards to repair his broken wall. We all go to our beds to rest up and heal. Before my father can go into his room I ask him about Warlord and his father. He tells me that mutants have always lived under us. Warlord's father Sin wants to destroy everyone on the surface so that the only beings left will be them, that way no one on the surface can torture them or kill them for no reason. When he was about my age Sin got a coo together and was going to try and kill everyone but his and Furrock's diligence paid off, they went in the middle of the night and killed Sin or so they thought.

"Warlord can be turned to our side, if his father is killed". He says. "This time it's not up to Furrock and I it's up to you kids. Warlord is too strong for you right now but soon he won't be…Trust me".

We give each other a hug and I leave the room. Realizing that I smell I go into the bathroom to take a shower the warm water feels so good against my skin. Looking at my body in the mirror I can see all the scars I have and I'm not even a quarter way into my life yet. Standing there looking at myself the reflection begins to morph into Kita.

"When I get through with you, you'll be dead". The reflection yells.

Shaking my head I look back into the mirror the only thing I can see is me.

When I get to my room Sounni is already sound asleep in our bed I get under the covers and hold Sounni as tightly as possible; she wakes up a little and holds me back. The night escapes us as we fall asleep holding each other.

The next day arrives and there's a knock at the door again. Instead of opening the door I wait for someone else to get it. My father comes into our room and tells me that Master Hiraski is in the kitchen waiting.

"Heard about what happened last night and a few days ago. Glad to see that my star pupil is doing all right".

"You want something from me or just here to visit"? I ask.

He informs us that he's here to see Jet and get some info on Warlord and Septh. My father tells him the story of Warlord's attack, also the story of his past and what happened with Sin, and the story of what Septh did to those AU soldiers.

"Unfortunately as strong as I am Septh would beat me in a few seconds". He says.

My father hands him the picture of our cousin being stabbed. Hiraski looks at it for a few seconds and puts it into his pocket. He commands us all to keep this under wraps, his reasoning is the fear for the people who would try to track him down and would end up dead. X is not happy with these results and speaks out of turn against Hiraski's decision.

"You want to get killed be my guest X but I will not put other Psychian's in danger". Hiraski argues.

Jet finally awakes from his sleep and sees Hiraski sitting in the kitchen.

"Hey, what's with all the commotion"? He asks.

"Jet, did you ever attend a Shogun school"? He asks.

Jet's head points towards the floor in disappointment. Hiraski walks over to him and directs him to walk with him outside for a bit. X asks me if I would like to spar with him for a little bit. When we go outside the three of us can see Shokon approaching. Apparently so can Master Hiraski because he stops suddenly when Shokon gets closer. Shokon as well stops from where he's at I can see his face is pale, as if he's seen a ghost. Before any our reflexes can react Hiraski has tackled Shokon and has his sword drawn.

"Traitor"! Hiraski yells.

X, Jet and I hold Hiraski's shoulders so that he cannot stab Shokon. Hiraski tells us that Shokon used to be his student but his intelligence has reported that he joined the Roko gang. Jet and I tell Hiraski that he evil no more. At first he fights the thought but then gets off of him.

"I'm watching you Shokon". Hiraski says coldly.

As X and I are sparring Furrock and my father come outside to sit on the porch. Concentrating on the fight and listening to them they talk about me fighting someone but never say the Psychian's name. X and I spar for a little bit until both of is satisfied. As we're walking back to the house Hiraski tells everyone that he has an announcement.

"Just a few minutes ago I assessed Jet's performance with his Shogun form and after seeing his skill in this form. It is with great honor that I will graduate him from his Shogun training". Hiraski announces.

Sorona and Sange come over to congratulate him on his success. When they're done Jet and I shake hands and nod our heads at each other. Just as my father and Furrock it is our mark of friendship.

After dinner we all gather around Jet and Hiraski for the small coronation. The room is full of candles and decorations for Jet who stands a few feet from Hiraski, who tells him to step forward and bow. Jet does as he's told and everyone in the room stares as Jet approaches. Today is Jet's day as though he may not have gone through the Shogun training, by heart he is one. Master Hiraski walks over to Jet and shakes his hand. When he does their hands light up, the sign that Jet has been graduated. A tear comes to Jet's eyes as rejoice sets in to his heart.

CHAPTER 16

NEW ATTACK

The next day we're all outside when Yamasaki appears a little outside of Furrock's house. He hands me the map with detailed instructions of where Krugnar lives. My father at first isn't too keen on the idea but he soon gives up on trying changing my mind. Asking Yamasaki why he won't just show me the way, he says nothing and goes on about his business.

Walking through the city the markets have started opening up again and the normal hustle and bustle is back to normal. When I get to his house there is a gate blocking all passages and barbed wire at the top of the fence. There is a button on the gate door, pressing it the button makes no noise. Assuming it's broken I keep pressing the button. The left side of the door opens up and a man steps out yelling.

"I'M TRYING TO HAVE Some pe…Oh, sorry Shinruga". He says.

His form seems a little sloppy and not to mention he's wearing sweat pants and a beater. To think that I have to teach him the Electric Psych Ball kind of sickens me. He tells me to come in and apologizes for the lack of formality.

We go into his living area where there are empty bottles of booze. Realizing that I can see the bottles he takes them into the kitchen.

"Don't worry I'm sober today". He says.

Looking around the place I can see pictures of him with some famous Psychian's, even one with Septh.

"You met Septh before"? I ask.

"Who do you think his father is kid"? Krugnar says.

At first I don't believe him but his story is hard not to believe. He reminds me that he's only his stepfather, Septh's real parents died when he was three years old and his mother a couple of months later from Gingereal. A disease that attacks your heart and lungs only named after the strongest woman fighter Ginger, who was half human half Psychian.

"I taught the kid everything he knows. His power I'm afraid is of natural selection". He says. "Soon not even I could control it and sent him on his way".

Telling him of the stories and how he's been acting Krugnar doesn't seem too surprised. As we sit there eating lunch I can't help myself, so I ask him what happened with Ikeya.

He stops eating and takes a sip of his tea. Krugnar begins telling me the story of what happened between the two of them. They were down in a secret cave under the school, at the end of a cave stood a large door. When the door opened Ikeya and Krugnar was ambushed by demon like creatures. They soon became overthrown by these creatures.

"How are you two still alive"? I ask.

"Ikeya and I were put in front of the creature's master. They blindfolded us for some reason, when he got off of his chair he asked us if we wanted to live or die". He tells.

Asking him how they survived he continues his story, Ikeya answered yes. If he is to live Ikeya would have to supply them with food. They only ate meat and people or Psychian's didn't matter to them. Ikeya accepted his offer so he was able to live.

"I refused to do his bidding and was dragged by two of the creatures into a cooking room, where they cuffed me up". He says. "Waiting for those monsters to leave I waited in the room while I was being cooked to death. When they did leave I used my energy to free myself. I tried to move the earth but for some reason it wouldn't budge".

He goes on to tell me that only having the few seconds left he used his energy to blast out of the room. When he did it was day time so the creatures couldn't chase him. The creatures master sent Ikeya to chase him.

"When we met on the surface Ikeya gave his reasoning for being the creatures slave". He says.

Tracking back in his mind Krugnar remembers the day as clear as day. I can see it in his eyes and hear it in his voice that speaking of this day makes him sad.

"Ikeya, why would you agree to do those creatures bidding"? Krugnar asks.

"To save my life, if the AU attack swearing my allegiance will mean life security. The Triple Psychian won't be around for another few years, the AU is not going to wait that long". He says.

"You're weak".

Krugnar goes on to finish his story that after he said that remark, Ikeya fired everything he's got. For Ikeya he made it look as though he was destroyed. Since that day he has had no trouble with anyone or anything. The dayof the battle Krugnar says he saw Ikeya but he soon vanished as he knew he would be hunted down till he was captured or dead.

After we are done eating lunch Krugnar leads me outside the backyard. It is beautiful with a huge garden and fountains.

"This is where you will teach me your attack". He says.

"If I may ask what is so important of teaching you this attack"? I ask him.

"The blade I possess is called the Amplifier blade, it amplifies attacks by twenty times their normal rate. By obtaining the strongest attacks in the world I become an arsenal of power". He says.

His point is clear and understandable but he sees the disappointment in my eyes.

"Tell you what as an added bonus I'll teach you a technique as well". He says.

My eyes light up at the thought of learning a new technique. I begin the first step of the two part move, using my energy I send lightning into the sky. When it comes down I begin focusing my energy but mess it up and the whole thing explodes in my face.

"That happens every once in a while". I say.

Krugnar asks when I used this move recently. I reply by telling him the two times I've used it so far, which was against Ikeya and Warlord.

"Savior moments, a time when you were under a lot of stress and my instincts kicked in". He explains.

He asks me to concentrate more and focus my brain on nothing but my attack. The obvious thing a Psychian should know when using an attack. Once again I summon the lightning and my energy but the same thing happens, the moves blows up in my face. Krugnar suggest that I add more lightning to the attack. So I wipe the soot from my face and try again with more lightning. This time the move works and I blast down one of his trees. He starts freaking out over me hitting the tree with my attack. His hands start going up and down in a frantic motion and he puts his head up against the tree.

"Did I do something wrong…Sir"? I ask him.

"THIS TREE HAS BEEN IN MY FAMILY FOR OVER FOUR HUNDRED YEARS". He yells. "Next time you want to fire attacks in someone's yard ask before you fire at any random thing.

Before Krugnar uses the attack I explain to him that he has to lace the middle of it with ten percent life energy. Somehow on his first attempt he uses the Electric Psych Ball with ease.

"Now for you to learn my move, it's called Fireworks". He yells in a macho voice.

The name of the attack brings disappointment into the air again.

"Oh, come on its better than it sounds". He assures me.

He asks me if I've ever been in a situation where a high distance multiple hitting attack would come in handy. Nodding my head he explains that this technique would help out dramatically.

After a few hours of training I walk back to Furrock's house excited to show everyone what I've learned. It takes me a few more minutes to get back to Furrock's house because on the way home I pass by a flower shop. The shop is filled with the biggest assortment of flowers I've ever seen.

"Hello, can I help you"? A charming lady asks me.

She has a hat on with flowers attached to them. Her eyes bug out of her head, at first I think they are going to fall out of her eye sockets. She tells me that they have every flower that grows in the world. Even a new one called the Dafidose, a hybrid flower from three separate ones. I pay for the flower at the front desk and on the way home, I decide to look it over some more. When I open the door Sounni wraps her arms around me and gives me the biggest kiss she can offer. I get into the kitchen and set the flower on the table. The second my dad walks into the kitchen and his eyes see the flower he reaches for the nearest sword and cuts the flower in half.

"Did you sniff the flower"? He asks.

"Yeah, why its"! He cuts me off.

"Did it open when you did"?

"No". I say.

I keep asking him what is the matter but he only walks over to the flower again and set it on fire. Trying to push my way through Furrock and my dad won't let me move.

"You see that black smoke from the flower its poison. If you sniff the flower and it opens the poison kills you five minutes later. They were created to silently kill people. It took a lot of time for people to figure murders out until this plant's creator finally took credit for it. If burned the poison is useless and non toxic". He explains.

He then asks me who sold it to me, telling him the shop name we rush over there. When we arrive the bug eyed woman is gone. Farther behind the counter there is a body of another girl with the middle of her throat stabbed. We leave the shop and tell an official what just conspired and they take care of the rest.

On the way back to Furrock's Sounni meets us halfway and thanks me for the consideration. Knowing that another person died because of me doesn't make her compliment warm my heart. Is this how it's always going to be, people dying at my feet because of the Brigidane blade and the power it contains. No I decide it's time to end this war and destroy the AU. Vengeance will be brought to those with family killed by the AU, by all means necessary.

CHAPTER 17

ELEMENKA ATTACK

Jet

It's a beautiful Friday morning and Sorona and I have a date together. She meets me outside of Furrock's house and we head off into town. Today will be a day of relaxation and rest, no fighting or war. A day for just Sorona and me in the market place we first find a place to sit down and eat. We stop at a little place called Betsie's sit and eat. The food is scrumptious but because of the battle a few weeks ago the food choices are limited as well as supplies. The whole town is hurting but will eventually make a recovery, after all it recovered once already.

Going down an alley there is a group of people dancing to some music. Before I can ask Sorona if she wants to dance she grabs my arm and pulls me onto the mat. As I'm standing there I realize that I don't know how to dance. Sorona grabs my hand and shows me how to do a move, she then tells me to repeat it. Doing so she shows me another one and I repeat. Soon the two of us are perfectly coordinated and enjoying ourselves. Saying goodbye to our new friends we depart for Furrock's house.

When we get into Furrock's house we're greeted by Sounni who has prepared a roast for us. Shinruga and X are mingling and Shokon will be arriving soon. We all get a laugh when Shinruga tries to balance many things at once and almost dropped the roast on the floor. We fall silent when Shinruga's Brigidane blade starts lighting up at the bottom of the handle.

"An Elemenka gem is near". He says.

We rush outside to see if any fighter is outside but can't see any. The three of us can't even feel the presence of someone nearby. Sorona comes out a few seconds later to help but we just go inside and finish eating. Sounni's food is really good, it usually is. She may not be Psychian but her specialty is definitely cooking. Sorona feels a little jealous when I compliment Sounni on all the food. Soon after dinner she departs for home, we kiss each other goodnight.

Shinruga is waiting in the kitchen for me, he tells me to follow her because the Brigidane blade lit up while I was outside. I run out the door to catch up her and when I do she jumps a little.

"What's wrong Jet"? She asks.

Telling her of the Brigidane blade lighting up she is immediately on guard.

"People could try to get to you through Shinruga and me, plus you've already been attacked once". I say.

She grabs my arm and holds me closer to herself. That's when I can feel it the presence of someone behind us, when I look there is no one.

"What's wrong"? Sorona asks.

"You didn't feel that"? I ask.

"If you're trying to freak me out its working, what are you talking about"?

Laughing like an idiot she reminds me that trying to scare her is not funny. Ignoring what I felt we press on till we get to her house. When we arrive her dad greets me at the door. He is a huge man and his fist look as though they could crush my head with one squeeze. I put my arms around Sorona and give her a hug and kiss. He gives me a stern look but before he can say or do anything I'm practically down the block. Once again on the way back I can feel the energy I felt. It's night time so every where there is a shadow. My eyes wander looking in all directions but still no one. As I'm walking a shadow forms behind mine but when I look there is nothing. After walking a few more feet it appears again but Shinruga appears ahead of me and it retreats.

"Did you see that"? I ask Shinruga.

"See what"? He asks.

I explain the shadow that I saw blocking my own. He tells me that he didn't see anyone but definitely felt someone's power. On guard for any sneak attacks we continue to walk to Furrock's house. When we get there I go to my room and immediately fall asleep when my head lands on the pillow.

The next day everyone but Shinruga is awake. Sounni tells me that he was up all night working on a new attack. When Shinruga wakes up I ask him to demonstrate his new move after breakfast. He scarf's his food down and runs out the door. Turning into Kimoshiran form he pulls his hand close to his hip and concentrates his energy. Putting his hand towards the sky the energy fires like a firework and explodes into pieces, the pieces that fall to the ground explode.

"Wow, that's pretty cool"! I yell.

"Krugnar described it as the AU eradicator". He tells us all.

Without warning Sorona grabs my arm and pulls me towards town. She tells me that there is a festival going on in town that honors the first Shiran battle. I notice that none of my other friends is coming to the festival with us. Sorona tells me that Yamasaki stopped by and wanted to talk to Shinruga, Shinsaga and Furrock, and they will catch up to us.

While walking through town Sorona notices that a person behind us has been following us for a while.

"Can we help you"? I ask.

He stops walking towards us and stares at us until we're bugged out.

"My name is Metallic and I have an Elemenka gem. I would like to fight to Shinruga".

Striking a deal with him is easy; I offer him the chance to have me as an slave if I can't beat him. His face is shiny more than normal persons should be. His facial expressions kind of creep us out as well, his eyes are wandering in all directions. If you look closer you can see that they're actually a deep red.

"Are you ready"? He asks.

The second the fight starts I charge and my fist lands a direct hit to his draw. Instead of Metallic flying or getting knocked down he stands there. My hand begins to swell as if I hit a sheet of metal.

"What the heck is his face made of"? I yell out in pain.

Hitting different spots on his body the same thing happens, instant pain. Metallic begins to chuckle at the expense of my pain. Staring him down I unsheathe my sword, he is instantly on guard.

"So regular attacks may not hurt you but it looks as though a sword might". I say.

Instead of pulling out a sword as I assumed he would he pulls out a little round piece of metal, when he holds it out it extends into a staff with pointed ends on each side. Charging his form is spectacular and he even knocks me to the ground but before he can stab me I roll out of the way. Firing a couple of blasts of energy he once again doesn't even try to dodge or block the attacks.

"Don't you get it; Metallic my skin is like metal any blunt or blasts attacks won't hurt me". He says.

I pull out my sword again and wait for the opportune moment. Staring at him the one thing I realize is that his power level is weak. The metal like body of his must be his biggest advantage. Not realizing it Metallic has burrowed a metal tentacle like thing underground, it comes from behind and starts choking me. As I sit there choking to death Sorona intervenes by shooting him with an energy arrow. He turns towards her and lets his grip go on my neck. My vision is blurry but I can see Metallic heading in Sorona's direction. Transforming into Kimoshiran form I use the K-gateway technique to appear behind him. Somehow he senses the attack and once again continues to choke me. He also makes another one that grabs Sorona by her stomach and begins to crush her.

"You can both die by each other". Metallic says laughing.

Sorona's screams make me think quickly, she's about to drop her sword. I tell her to drop the sword so that the bottom of the handle can touch my foot. When she does I push my foot, sending the blade into his spine. His grip on us loosens and he falls to his knees. As he sits there his eyes are wide open and he has his staff held tight.

"Here take it I'm finally free". Metallic says.

The Elemenka gem falls to the ground in front of him and I pick it up. His eyes seem normal now as he asks me for an honorable death. He says though that he would like to make one more request, a warning he tells. His last words as he dies are faint and hard to hear but I get the point of it.

"The Sin of all will come for Shinruga and then nothing will save you". He says faintly.

Right as Sorona's blade comes swinging horizontally and then his head bounces on the ground, as Metallic last words are spoken.

I'm not sure what he means but Shinruga is in danger.

Shinruga

The Brigidane blade got broke by the last Elemenka gem holder that had escaped. Being in the shower always calms my mind so I soak in the hot water. It's a place where I can just sit and think with no worries. When I get out Furrock tells me that Yamasaki is waiting outside for me. Before I can even speak he hands me a map. He explains that this map is the location of where the Triple Psychian tournament will be held. Once again before I can say anything he's off. Looking at the back of the map I notice some writing.

"Don't go the other way". The note reads.

At first I'm confused but I soon realize that the meaning is telling me to stay on the side of good.

Looking down the road I notice Jet running towards me, when he gets closer I notice that Sorona has a mark on her neck. He hands me an Elemenka gem and explains what happened today in town. Thanking him I put the gem close to the bottom of the sword handle. The bottom of the handle begins glowing and the surge of energy is intense.

Now there are only two more Elemenka gem holders out there, first you guys and then the AU.

CHAPTER 18

MEMORIES RETURN

The weeks pass by as the beginning of our Shogun training is going to be starting soon. My dad left a few days along with so that he may complete his Psychian Warrior training. It's now time to get going seeing as though getting to Saya will take a week or two. Since Sange and Sorona have not completed their Shogun training either the three of us are going to Hiraski's school to train. X will be attending the same school I did when I went through Psychian Warrior, Sochajo will be teaching him. Jet is going to a school in New Haven a wondrous city said to be where the first Psychian Warrior was born.

In the kitchen we're all eating our last meal together as friends and family. When we are done eating Sange and Sorona go back home to get the rest of their supplies. Jet and I also pack up the rest of our few belongings and our supplies. The two of us wait outside for Sange and Sorona to return, they finally do with their backpacks full. It's nearing dusk now and we say goodbye to our friends and loved ones.

"You come back my love. I would like to keep my husband to be". Sounni whispers.

"Don't worry I'll be back". I say.

"I love you". She replies.

"I love you to my love".

Sounni and Sorona hug each other and Sounni whispers something in her ear but I can't my ears can't figure out what she said. Sounni hugs

Jet and Sange as well reminding them to be careful. Sounni and I kiss one more time before we depart from each other once again.

We're just out of town and I stop for a second to look over the town of Shiran. Most of it looks the same but the parts that got the worst of the battle a few weeks ago are noticeable. The four of us stare at the city for a few minutes and then we start our new journey. I pull out the map that Yamasaki gave to me showing the location of where the Triple Psychian tournament will be held. Jet comes over to me and asks if he can take a look at it. He looks as though he's studying the map and the location.

During our first couple of days of travel there is no sign of anyone on our tail or anyone who wants to fight us. When we stop to ask an old man for directions he surprises us by trying to stab me but he's so old at half my normal speed I could have dodged his attack. After knocking him to the ground the old man's son rushes over to me. He tells us that he's got a serious case of dementia and doesn't know human from Psychian or a rock from a person.

After a few hours of walking we find a suitable location to set camp. Sange and I collect the wood for the fire, while Sorona and Jet fetch a deer for dinner. As we're sitting there Jet and Sorona are snuggled close to each other while Sange and I eat our dinner in peace. That's when I can feel a presence behind me but when I look back there is no one there.

"What is it Shinruga"? Jet asks.

"Nothing"! I say.

This power that I felt feels so familiar but I can't peg whose it is. Ignoring who is out there I finish my dinner and go to sleep. Occasionally getting up to check the fire and chucking a couple of pieces of wood in it, the presence I felt is no longer around.

A different dream then usual plagues my mind, this time my dream is about the night my sister left the house.

"Stay out of my way father". My sister yells.

She fires a blast right into his gut and bolts out the door. I can still remember that night as if it were yesterday. The rest of the night my body is restless and I don't get much sleep.

The morning sun is now rising over the horizon and the four of us is already packed and on our way. We head in the direction of Saya only to find more horrors along the way. As it nears the afternoon we come across a village with all dead and the place still burning from the flames. Looking closer this doesn't appear to be a forest fire or an act of Mother Nature it looks as though Psychian's had caused this fire.

We get to a fork in the road and the four stop. Jet turns towards Sorona and gives her a kiss on the cheek and then the lips. He then gives Sange a hug, and turns towards me we do our usual handshake and then we hug.

"You take care of yourself man, don't get into any trouble". I remind him.

"I could say the same to you, we both got girls to return to". He says.

We nod and say our last goodbyes as our friend disappears from our sight but not our minds.

It's nearing dusk now and that's when I sense that same person again. The three of us are looking in all directions, so I'm guessing that Sorona and Sange can sense them two. We get closer to the There is rustling in the trees behind us, as I get closer a red dot flickers. Soon a machine comes out of the woods and then there is more of them. The top of them is square with a lens in the middle and their legs are only an inch thick. The three of us stare at the machines in amazement but soon take cover. The machines tops open up to reveal an assortment of weapons. Defeating the machines is easy whether we attack from the front or behind we take them out as if they are toys. There is another rustling from the woods again, this time a troop of AU soldiers appear. Leading the troop is a Psychian girl whose power feels so familiar. The Psychian girl holds out her left hand and pushes a button on her wrist, the robots begin climbing on each other and then form an enormous robot. Sange, Sorona and I are about ready to attack but the Psychian orders me to leave the robot and fight her. The AU soldiers attack but I easily defeat them.

"Why, who are you"? I ask.

The Psychian simply waves her hand taunting me to fight her. Her body is wrapped in light armor and her head has a cloak around it, I don't see much of a point to the cloak. She waves her hand once more to fight, I charge at her and she deflects the energy blast I've fired. She pulls out her sword or so I think the only thing I can see is the hilt. When I get up to her and slash the first attack connects but the rest seem to strike only air. The searing pain goes down my back as a blade strikes my back. The Masked Psychian girl stands over me as she fills her hand with energy. Rolling out of the way I'm surprised when I stand up my enemy uses the Implosion box technique around me. Quickly changing into Kimoshiran form I use the K-gateway attack to teleport out of the attack. Taking a quick second to get my head on I can see that Sange and Sorona is having trouble with the machine. Turning back into Psychian Warrior form I reface my enemy. I throw energy up into the sky and summon the lightning to power up my Electric Psych Ball. Somehow she knows this attack to because when I summon the lightning her eyes light up. Shooting the blast she easily dodges the attack.

"I'm surprised you know that attack but you missed by a lot". She gloats.

"Who says I was trying to hit you"? I say.

When she looks back she can see that the robot has a big chunk missing out of it.

"Clever, but it can survive". She informs me.

"Not if I hit the part of it that can't survive a hit from electricity". I brag.

The girl puts a shield up to her back and lets out a little chuckle. The robot stands for a few more seconds and then explodes. Sorona and Sange become engulfed by the flames or so I thought.

"You aren't the only one who learned the K-Gateway". Sorona says.

The masked fighter charges at the three of us, she instantly targets me. With the strength I have left defending against her is no easy task. Sorona tries to step in but the Psychian girl strikes Sorona with her knee. The hit makes Sorona drop to the ground. She knocks Sange out of the way and fills her hand with a lot of energy. The energy is glowing bright in my face and just when I think I'm done for someone tackles her to the ground. The blast she had prepared in her hand flies into a group of trees and obliterates them into pieces. When I look up Yamasaki is over top of the Psychian girl trying to pound her face into the ground but she kicks him off of her.

"You think she's strong enough"? I remark.

"Why don't you show him you are…Kela"? He says.

The Psychian girl takes her cloak off to reveal her face. It can't be no, she's supposed to be dead.

"Hello, Shinruga". She says.

I collapse to the ground and wrap my arms around my stomach. Sorona runs to me and tries to hold me up but I can't summon any strength. My limbs are like jell-o and they won't support the rest of my body.

"Who is Kela and what is wrong Shinruga"? Sorona asks.

"Kela is Shinruga's older sister". Explains Yamasaki.

"I'm glad to see you again little brother. Father must be so proud of you". She says.

To assure myself that it's her, I look at her face. The dark concentrated eyes and the side bang comb to the left, ponytail in the back. The only thing different is the scar on her left eye.

Yamasaki tells us that he's been tracking her for a while and she's been around the whole time. Everybody told me she was dead, why did they lie to me? My brain races till the only thing inside is anger and the thought of killing her. My energy starts flowing out of my body the dark purple energy flares and the air fills pressured. I yell out in rage powered up and ready for battle.

"Ah, this should be interesting Shinruga". She says.

I charge and throw a fury of fist but it's as though my attacks have no effect. She kicks me to my gut and is about to stab me again but Yamasaki throws a shuriken and hits her hand. Sorona and Sange tag team her and knock her to the ground. Kela spins on the ground releasing energy in all directions close to her. Sorona falls to the ground, Kela pursues her but Yamasaki blocks her attack again.

"Yamasaki, you're such a pest". Kela yells.

Powering up again I pursue after my sister who's fighting with Yamasaki. Her power and skills are amazing as she easily can hold up her own against the two of us. Sange fires off a blast from afar, Yamasaki and I step out of the way for Sange's attack. Kela throws her hands up and blocks the attack, Sange cranks up the juice. Realizing that at this rate Sange's attack could be diverted I fire a blast at his trying to make it explode. Kela senses the blast coming, she summons a piece of earth that goes in front of Sange's blast. When my blast connects the piece of earth explodes as well as Sange's attack.

"She used the earth to make lessen the damage she would have taken". Yamasaki says.

Yamasaki apologizes for not telling me about Kela because he was under strict orders not to release the information. Kela finally rises from the ground but she doesn't look that hurt. Sange and I charge again but she disappears before our eyes. In a flash she shows up from our side and attacks. He knocks Sange to the ground and is about to finish him when Sorona's blade comes down behind Kela. Somehow Kela's blade is already there. Sorona kicks Kela to the ground and fires a blast but she disappears again.

"Its mirrors you guys they blend into their background and she can go into anyone of them and come out of them and attack". Yamasaki yells.

The four of us put our backs to each other and wait for her to attack. At first I see nothing but in between one of the mirrors I catch her feet.

"There that one"! I yell.

We all focus our energy onto that mirror and fire an attack. Kela comes from my front but I act as if I'm scared to move. Sorona uses the K-gateway to come from her right but Kela's senses detect her and she avoids the attack.

"Ha, you think that silly attacks like that will work you fool". She gloats. "Wait there was fo".

Yamasaki attacks from the left before she can finish her sentence. His fist lands hard as Kela goes flying across the battlefield.

The four of us rejoice but not for too long. Kela gets up quicker than anticipated, she powers up some energy and makes a giant mirror. The mirror flies over my three friends and captures them.

"The mirror will continue to crush them unless you can either defeat me or break it". Kela chuckles.

Yamasaki tries to move the earth under the ground to sink into but it's no good the box is underground as well.

"What do we do I've tried the K-gateway it doesn't work in here". Sorona says.

Turning back into Kimoshiran form I run over to the box but before I reach it, Kela gets in my way. Using the K-gateway I teleport to several areas of the box, trying to break the box I find no weak points. Finally Kela finds a way to keep up with me. The box is getting closer to my friends, I can see the desperation looming over their head. They are now lying down to escape being crushed.

Knowing that this could be the last chance I have to save my friends I charge with all my energy. Saying my goodbyes to my family and friends, I knowingly will sacrifice my life for them. Kela puts out her energy filled hands to defend my attack.

"I DON'T CARE IF I DIE JUST AS LONG AS MY FRIENDS ARE SAFE"! I yell.

Our hands and power collide; the energy levels are so powerful lightning begins to shoot out.

"Die you fool". Kela yells.

We're at a stalemate when Kela summons lightning in her hand to make an Electric Psych Ball. Being in Kimoshiran form I cannot use that attack. Using the K-gateway technique would be too risky at the moment. Using that technique could send the EPB into the dimension with me where I would be obliterated.

Hearing my friends screaming sends even more anger through my body, I push my energy forward. Kela begins to back up a little but regains her balance, Sorona's screams push me over the edge. My energy begins to change color from blue to a bluish orange color. Kela can't push back the energy is too strong for her.

"You're through". I yell feeding more energy into my attack.

The energy turns completely orange and sends Kela flying and her glass box shattering. My friends regain their footing and we use the K-gateway attack to surround Kela.

"Anyone knows when they're beaten". She says.

Just when the four of us think she's beaten Kela throws a dart. She hits me in the chest and runs a few feet before stopping.

"That poison will kill him about ten hours". She says.

Yamasaki's anger gets the best of him and he fires most of his energy into one blast, it clears the trees out but no Kela can be seen. The poison kicks in immediately and my body begins to feel hot and weak, Yamasaki informs us that the school is only a mile away. Sange loads me on to his back and begins walking but we're all pretty tired from our battle. As they try to rush me to the school I wonder will I make what will happen if I don't the thought race through my mind. How will Sounni live without me, would've I been the Triple Psychian if I'd had lived through this battle. A little away from the school Sange trips on something and I go tumbling to the ground but my muscles are too weak to stand.

"Shinruga, hold on the school is right there, don't close your eyes. Stay with me friend". Yells Yamasaki.

My eyes catch Sorona with tears in her eyes but she tries not to show them.

The darkness now consumes my eyes is it forever or maybe for a short time?

About the Author

Since I was a little kid writing and drawing took up a lot of my time. English was the only class I could pass really, pretty much failed the other ones. Writing came easy to me though and as I got older my imagination stayed, luckily or else this book would have never been wrote.

Michigan has been my home for almost my whole life. I will be twenty two years old in about two weeks and married on October 1st to my lovely fiancée Bethany Walker. Eventually my hopes is that this book is made into a cartoon and put on the Nickelodeon network.